Praise for Elliott Murphy's

Poetic Justice

I0658733

Figaro

The most literary of the great american rock composers, on the same level as Dylan or Leonard Cohen, always fascinated by the image of F Scott Fitzgerald, the author of inspired albums ... has finally thrown himself into the world of novels.

Temoignage Chretien

Like six bullets from a pistol, or the seven orignal sins, the story shifts between [old Oklahoma] and decadent New York; whores with hearts of gold, damned poets, elegant bandits, defrocked priests, lyrical gangsters, dishonest sheriffs ... A western dressed as a dark thriller. Very *noir.*

Livres Hebdo

After the short stories of *Café Notes*, the singer Elliott Murphy returns strongly with a literary western worthy of John Ford.

Inrockuptibles

Poetic Justice without a doubt ... the story of Elliott Murphy, the American songwriter and novelist living in exile in Paris since fifteen years, ... comes together show his love of country in a fresco of pre-modern America. A epic story told from the angle of individual destiny, through the very accurate portraits of lost sons and daughters.

ELLIOTT MURPHY
Poetic Justice

Elliott Murphy is the author of *Cold and Electric*, a rock 'n' roll novel excerpted in *Rolling Stone* magazine and published in French, German & Italian editions, as well as numerous published collections of short stories. Also an acclaimed singer/songwriter, he has released over thirty albums in his musical career and continues to tour and play concerts all over the world. He lives in Paris, France with his wife and son.

www.elliottmurphy.com

Elliott Murphy is available for lectures, readings and concerts. For information regarding his availability, please contact: info@elliottmurphy.com

ALSO BY ELLIOTT MURPHY

Cold And Electric
Café Notes
Where The Women Are Naked And The Men Are Rich
The Lion Sleeps Tonight
The Red General

SELECTED DISCOGRAPHY

Aquashow
Night Lights
Selling the Gold
Beauregard
Strings of the Storm
Notes from the Underground
Elliott Murphy

For the late Kevin McShane, once upon a time my manager, agent, confidant and above all, faithful friend, with gratitude. I dreamed big and you always kept the faith. Miss you Mister McShane.

POETIC JUSTICE

A Novel by Elliott Murphy

"Great are the myths...I too delight in them!"

- *Walt Whitman*

Books

PART ONE: PETIT JEAN

Vendee, Old Oklahoma 1883

Chapter 1

At thirteen and a half Petit Jean O'Keefe already had a sense that some men carried evil within them, its presence as steadfast as a heartbeat. And when he had entered the dim saloon that drizzly afternoon trailing behind his father to see the filthy Carpis standing by the bar, boots and spurs caked in mud and horseshit, it had scared all that's holy out of the boy. With a choking, metallic taste of fear in his mouth, Petit Jean began to tremble and he tugged at his father's sleeve and asked him please, let's not go in there, not in this bar with that man standing there; why not just leave now and get on home to his ma and sister waiting on them back at the farm. But his pa kept walking right into the saloon, not even looking at the boy and told Petit Jean to set himself down in a corner for a spell, assuring the boy they'd only stay in the saloon for a very short while.

"Just wanting to celebrate the sale of me pigs, you know. Nothing wrong with that is there?"

Eyes to the floor, Petit Jean trailed behind his father as they entered into the dark recesses of the saloon where Carpis slumped down on the low bar, resting his chin on his elbows, his torn pants and chaps riding below his girth, the dark crack of his ass circumvented by his gun belt. Eyeing Petit Jean's father with a cold, unsmiling stare Carpis spat on the floor when John O'Keefe told the barkeep to bring him a bottle of his better stock of whiskey. Petit Jean slouched down in the corner of the musty room and nervously fidgeted with the wooden pistol his father had carved for him that he kept always tucked in his pants. The toy gun was worn smooth and dark now from endless hours playing bandits: him, a brave Jesse James facing down shifty Pinkerton detectives in the form of a few stray hogs back on their farm. Petit Jean knew his ma would skin both of them if she knew where they were that late afternoon, in that saloon, but he tried not to think about that.

His pa quickly poured and downed two shots of whisky and then pulled out a wad of bills from the pocket of his blue Union coat. He turned around and slapped the money on top of the round poker table behind him, money that had been in his possession for less than quarter of an hour after selling his six pigs. When he smiled and proclaimed, "By God, I feel lucky today!", the boy began to tremble even more and was gripped with a dreadful sense of premonition, fearing that his father's boasting was some sure way of tempting the fates to visit them with something terrible.

Small herds of cattle and their mounted drivers strolled by in the drizzling rain that muddied the packed earthen trail outside the small saloon's doors. Red coals in the big bellied iron stove popped and hissed and Jack Blankets, the scar faced Cherokee Indian, silently took his usual place squatting next to the warm stove, saying nothing, his arms folded in front of him and his brightly woven blanket drawn high over his shoulders. For half an hour or so it was just another low stakes friendly poker game with John O'Keefe playing and joking with two cowboys come in from the rain and it seemed Petit Jean's pa was doing better than breaking even, the pile of loose coins in front of him growing with nearly every hand. Carpis watched the game intently from his end of the crude bar - two long wooden planks roped together and laid over upturned barrels – sometimes spitting a long string of tobacco juice in the direction of the spittoon, which only swung back on him adding another greasy stain to his already long gone jersey. Either out of embarrassment at his lack of spitting prowess or just from some recalled sense of mission he abruptly quit the saloon in a clumsy, hurried step. The three card players all looked up for a moment as Carpis' spurs clattered out of the place.

"Reckon it was time for his yearly bath," said John O'Keefe. But neither cowboy laughed along with him, not getting the joke – neither of them being too pristine in their own personal hygiene.

"Mighta been just that," said one of the cowboys in earnest.

A half hour later when Petit Jean looked up to see the tall figure of Judge Durand pushing open the swinging doors of the saloon and haughtily surveying its few customers, he was gripped with an even more gut wrenching sense of dread but he felt powerless to move, to do anything. He was transfixed as he watched Judge Durand enter the lowdown place like it was just another parcel of his own domain, beholding and frowning down on the card players, as if only he could dictate who might have the right to play some hands of poker at that table. Petit Jean could not figure out how a man could be so proud and evil at once. Right behind Judge Durand stood the filthy Carpis, grinning like hell from ear to ear, picking his nose.

"Is this a closed deal or might a gentleman sit in for a few turns of the deck?" Durand demanded of no one in particular and without waiting for a reply and with Carpis following dog's length behind him, he sat right down at the round table and was quickly dealt a hand by the cowboy holding the cards.

Slowly, without looking up from his cards, John O'Keefe spoke: "All men are free now Judge," he said. "Reckon you can sit where you like." Petit Jean cringed when he heard his father provoke these two men in such a way but he was powerless to stop him. "You do remember who won the war, don't you, your honor?" his pa added contemptuously. "I guess Abe Lincoln even included folks like you in the Emancipation Proclamation." The cowboys did laugh at that, believing John O'Keefe banter was all in good fun.

"That I do," said Durand in his lofty southern accent. "And believe me sir, although the war may be over for some the cause will never die in me as I have never reneged on my pledge to the Confederacy nor acknowledged the shameful surrender of General Lee, which still rests heavily on my soul."

With those words the Judge laid his hand grievously over his heart; but judging by his sartorial splendor and arrogant manner it did not appear that anything was weighing particularly heavy on the Judge's soul or fortune either for that matter. Judge Durand was easily the best-dressed man in the Indian territories, perhaps the only well dressed man in Vendee, and rumored to be the richest as well. For even on this drizzly

6

April day Durand was clad in a finely tailored New Orleans riding suit with a starched, frilly linen shirt and a blue silk foulard. Why he chose to keep up the pretense of such vanity in a territory where mirrors themselves were a rarity and where a man's conceit, if he had any at all, was better measured by his persistence to survive in a land already well inhabited by Indians, blizzards and uncertainty was plain ludicrous. But Judge Abel Durand would travel two towns over into Arkansas once a month for a haircut and a shave and he tromped around the meager town of Vendee in well shined cavalry boots, complete with shiny spurs, come rain or shine.

Whether Durand was really a judge in any legal sense at all was strictly a matter of whose opinion you chose to believe, there being little way of checking credentials west of the Mississippi. The Judge himself insisted that he had presided over the municipal court of the city of New Orleans before the treasonous laws of reconstruction were enacted but him being a decorated veteran of the Confederate Army, northern carpetbaggers and scalawags had conspired to unfairly throw him off his own judicial bench in a rigged election. Such *rigging*, in the judge's opinion consisting of giving former slaves the right to vote. But still other folks hinted that a darker reason had made Durand quit Louisiana, forcing him to leave the gentility of the French Quarter and hightailing it out to the Indian Territories where gentility, along with everything else but space - and Indians - was in short supply.

Carpis, on the other hand was everything the judge was not: a filthy, bent little man with rotting brown teeth who followed the judge like a faithful, mangy dog, never more content than when he was able to do the judge's dirty work, be it throwing tenant farmers off their land or ambushing suspected rustlers. It was surprising that someone with as delicate sensibilities as the judge could even stand to constantly associate with such a revolting figure as Carpis, a man who when folks happened to stroll up wind of him, often caused them to hold their kerchiefs over their nose and shake their heads in disbelief that any human being could smell so vile.

For a while, a rousing, seemingly cordial card game ensued between John O'Keefe, the two cowboys, Judge Durand and Carpis. Even Doc Rushman, the local *sawbones*, stopped by and joined in for a few hands. Then the cowboys departed to re-join their herd already headed up the Chisholm Trail to Wichita, and Doc Rushman, after declaring he had lost enough for one day, took off as well. Now the game was down to John O'Keefe, Judge Durand and Carpis and the bar itself was nearly empty - even the barman having ducked out to the outhouse at back of the saloon for an extended nature's call. All at once Petit Jean's pa began losing nearly every hand and within less than an hour of play, all the money from the sale of his pigs had gone completely over to the other side of the table in front of Judge Durand. John O'Keefe's naturally crimson Irish complexion was becoming darker and even redder and he visibly maddened with each deal of the cards until finally, when he had lost his last precious dollar, he threw his cards on the table and declared:

8

"Something ain't right here, these cards ain't falling like they should be."

The Judge, stroking his silver goatee and looking bemusedly over to his man Carpis, calmly asked John O'Keefe: "Are you sir, accusing anyone in particular of cheating? Because where I come from a gentlemen accepts the luck of the draw without turning to such sorry accusations to make up for his own lack of deftness at the gaming table."

Both Durand and John O'Keefe leaned back in their chairs, hands inches from their gun belt, eyeing each other warily. The contrast between the two men was sorely plain: Durand a severe portrait of class, power and prestige and John O'Keefe just another struggling union veteran trying to work his farm and raise a family. No one would ever suspect by looking at the two men who had been on the winning side of the Civil War and whose side had been vanquished. Now, John O'Keefe might have had a volatile Irish temper on occasion but he wasn't fool enough to not appreciate his defenseless situation, being alone and outgunned in that bar with Durand and Carpis on either side of him and his young son sitting alone in the corner. He tried as best he could without losing face to tone down his accusation, even managing a slight smile.

"I ain't accusing anyone of anything in particular, Judge. I'm just saying that something ain't right with these cards, that's all. And I'm through with this goddamn game for today if you don't mind." With that John O'Keefe stood up and walked away from the table.

But Judge Durand was not about to let it go so easily, even though he had already won all of John O'Keefe's money.

"Sir, in New Orleans where my family has lived for generations it is customary that when one gentlemen accuses another gentlemen of cheating than there is a matter of honor which must be settled until satisfaction is obtained by the damaged party. Isn't that so Mister Carpis?" He looked at Carpis who opened his mouth of rotting teeth and grinned wide.

"Sure is, Judge. That's the way I always heard it was down there," said Carpis, barely able to control his fiendish giggles.

But John O'Keefe just kept walking away from the table. "Well New Orleans and all that goes on down there can go to the devil as far as I'm concerned," he said. "I'm taking my boy home." As he approached the corner where Petit Jean was sitting and playing with his wooden six-shooter, a bullet whizzed close by his ear. John O'Keefe immediately dropped to a crouch, pulling the heavy Colt Navy 45 out from his pants belt and turning around to see the judge standing in a stiff dueling stance at the far end of the bar, his smoking pistol outstretched before him.

"Why you son of a bitch!" John O'Keefe hollered. "You nearly shot me in the back." He brushed his ear, looking down at his hand to see if the bullet had creased him but found no trace of blood. "Christ, you better go take some shooting lessons before you go fighting any more duels, your Honor, because more than likely you're gonna meet a man someday whose gonna shoot back!" John O'Keefe laughed but at the same time kept the judge covered with his pistol and ducked down his head for an instant to say to his boy, "Jean, get outside and…"

"Shoot the bastard!" screamed Durand as he dropped to the floor and ducked beneath the gaming table.

The boy had already started to stand up and move toward the door when a shot rang out behind him and Petit Jean immediately outstretched his wooden pistol in front of him, then turned to see his father's heavy gun tumble to the floor with a solid thud as he put both of his hands to his stomach, his face grimacing with pain. Next to the poker table, cowering behind a chair, knelt Carpis who stood up smiling and giggling, his own smoking gun outstretched in front of him, held in both of his shaking hands.

"I got 'em for you judge. I sure got him!" Carpis yelled. Durand crawled out from under the table and immediately saw the implications of the situation and moved quickly to Carpis and switched guns with him.

"I admire your bravery Mr. Carpis, but anyone can see it was my shot which killed the backshooter," announced Durand, quickly twirling around to see if anyone was within hearing range. "Its as plain as day, he drew on me when my back was to him. Isn't that right Mr. Carpis? You being the sole witness to such treachery as happened here today."

"Just like you says, Judge. Nobody gonna say no different," answered Carpis. "It's like you says."

John O'Keefe sat down hard on the floor, his face blanched and painful spasms beginning in his chest. Petit Jean stood frozen for a minute clutching his wooden pistol before running to his father's side. "Pa! Pa! Are you all right, Pa?"

11

Judge Durand took three long strides to where John O'Keefe clutched at his wound and stood above him. "I guess that will be a lesson to keep rabble like you from accusing a gentlemen of cheating."

John O'Keefe could hardly talk. "Leave me be...leave me be here with my boy."

But the judge wouldn't stop. "It will take more than a mere war to stop a white southern gentlemen from standing up for his reputation when insulted by Union rabble." Then he kicked John O'Keefe squarely in the stomach and the blood began gushing out. "And insisting upon the justice that this damned territory needs so bad."

The boy aimed his wooden six-shooter up at the judge. "Leave us be! Leave my pa be!"

The judge laughed at the boy, and walked out of the saloon with Carpis in tow. Petit Jean was kneeling on the floor with his father's head in his lap. They were alone in the bar, The Indian Jack Blankets having disappeared at the first sign of trouble between white men. The boy tried to stop the blood pouring out of off his father with his hands, which quickly turned crimson.

"Petit Jean..." John O'Keefe barely croaked the words out: "You tell your ma...I'm so sorry." Then in a moment of terrible, tortuous silence, the boy's world stopped spinning and he sat motionless, still clinging to the last words of his father's farewell, waiting for another sound. And then John O'Keefe's eyes rolled up into their sockets and from his throat came the most horrible gurgling sound. It was a death rattle Petit Jean would recall with a shudder nearly every day for the rest of his life.

Chapter 2

The raw clapboard exterior of the Vendee saloon gave it an appearance more like a flat roofed tool shed than any kind of drinking or gaming establishment; its only feeble try for elegance or style being its ornate carved swinging doors, imported from St. Louis. And the round poker table that John O'Keefe had found so inviting had served more often then not as a makeshift operating theater where Doc Rushman had sewed up the more serious bullet wounds for over ten years when called in from his small storefront office down the street. But by the time Doc Rushman had arrived back at the saloon, it was too late for any doctor to undo what had been done to John O'Keefe who was all bled out as witnessed by the encircling violet stain spread out beneath his corpse onto the sawdust below. Petit Jean had held his father's lifeless body in his arms for what seemed like an eternity while Judge Durand took his own sweet time to inform the doctor that a man lay wounded who might need attending to. The doctor stood there helpless, holding his probes and stitching thread and needle unused in his hands. John O'Keefe was long gone from this world when he arrived to find Petit Jean kneeling on the floor cradling his dead father's head, rocking back and forth and murmuring to himself. John O'Keefe's eyes in a dead freeze, stuck wide open, staring into nothingness and the boy breathing hard, visibly traumatized and covered with his father's blood. Gently, Doc Rushman knelt down and pressed his ear against John O'Keefe's chest, listening in vain for the slightest sound from   his heart. Then he shook his head to the small crowd who had followed him to the saloon and closed the dead man's eyes with two fingers, turning toward the boy who still clutched at the blood soaked union coat his pa was wearing. Doc Rushman was a practical man of science, a veteran frontier doctor with few airs of sentimentality, who dispersed an encouraging or doomed prognosis with equal gravity. But as he looked down at the boy there, who stared back at him like he had the power of God himself, he was well aware of the enormity of what he was about to say and so he hesitated for a moment before swallowing hard and then saying softly: "I'm sorry son, your pa's gone." But the boy's expression didn't change and he didn't begin to cry as the doctor had expected.

A rider was sent out to the farm to fetch Petit Jean's ma while Doc Rushman summoned some men to lift John O'Keefe up onto the poker table where his corpse was covered with a tarpaulin to await the arrival of his widow. Petit Jean would not move from his father's side and he stood vigil, solemnly standing next to his father's body, looking at that big round gambling table, and thinking what a waste to have such a thing in a town like Vendee where so few townsfolk really had any money to gamble with anyway. As with any victim of a tragedy, his mind tried to turn back the time and change the course of events that had led here to this dreadful conclusion: he tried to imagine his pa passing that saloon by, not going in - and the two of them now on their way back to the farm where the smell of his ma's savory cooking would greet them as they opened the door to their small plains home. Then, with all the family sat down at the table for midday dinner, his pa would be telling him oft-repeated stories of the ferocious three day battle of Gettysburg which he loved to hear while his ma served roast pork with prunes. He could almost taste it…but then he slammed back into the horrible reality of what had happened, seeing father's body lying stiff under a cloth on that damned poker table, never again to tell dinnertime stories to his boy.

Hours later when Petit Jean turned to see his mother and baby sister standing at the door of the saloon, the pain and grief inside of him became so enormous, so overwhelming, and acute that he thought he might explode into a thousand drops of tears right then and there.

Nearly a month after the shooting the appointed Federal Marshall of the Territory arrived to conduct an official inquest into the death of John O'Keefe. Rose O'Keefe dressed her two children in what might euphemistically be called their *Sunday best* and tried to scrub some of the prairie dirt off her own tired, tear-stained face, putting on a somber, most recently sewn, black widow's shawl. In their innocence and in their shared grief, the family had buoyed themselves in some fashion by depending on this official process, this *inquest*, to give some sense of justice, some kind of meaning they might comprehend to the loss of a husband and father. For sure, tragedy was always close at hand on the frontier: children might be swept away by Cholera or the pox and Comanche could slaughter a whole family in a night's raid. But even in tragic misfortunes such as these there was still a grudged acceptance that such terrible events lay within the natural order, that this was the high price frontier life sometimes demanded for its precious promise of freedom and the nobility of owning ones own land and being beholden to no man.

But the circumstances that took John O'Keefe from his family still needed clarity and judgment, some place in the natural order of things, no matter how random and unfair that structure might be, and the family had been counting on this official hearing to bring a measure of relief from their terrible burden of grief, although not really knowing how it might or why it should.

Dan Barkin, one of half a dozen Federal Marshalls, who covered a huge swath of territory under their jurisdiction and whose only symbols of authority were a tarnished badge and a rarely opened volume of the last written federal laws, arrived in Vendee on a dusty spring afternoon swatting away the black flies that swarmed by his horses ears with a broken twig from a low-hanging Pine tree. From what he knew of the shooting of John O'Keefe he was already half convinced that it was no thing more then a hotheaded shooting over a game of Poker; an event not uncommon in his rounds. Anyway, it would be difficult for him or even a Federal Judge to prove guilt or innocence in such a dispute and he was damn sure that the official inquest he would half-heartedly perform this day was a waste of his own time and travel, having detoured him in the midst of hunting down a murderous crew of renegades last seen galloping toward the Canadian River. But that was before he met Judge Abel Durand.

The judge caught up with Dan Barkin in the livery stable while the

Marshall examined his horse. The lawman was tall and lanky in his mid-thirties with a drooping black handlebar moustache and a plug of tobacco frequently wedged in the corner of his jaw; a man who would surely rather spit out tobacco juice than waste words; words being things he had little use for or finesse with.

"You are Marshall Barkin, I presume?" Durand asked by way of introduction.

"That'd be me," said Barkin, straightening up with considerable effort, having been bent over his horse for some time now while examining a splintered right hoof.

"Sir, I am Judge Abel Durand and I have been informed by my associates that you have arrived in Vendee to perform some sort of official inquiry into the death of John O'Keefe and that you have scheduled a hearing for this afternoon. Is my information correct, sir?"

It was rare that anybody addressed Dan Barkin as "sir" and that alone was enough to make the Marshall leery of this southern dandy who stood next to him with a gloved hand held to his nose to defray the smells of the stable.

"Well, I don't know your *associates* from a hill of beans but yes, there will be a hearing held in that there saloon this afternoon so I can report my findings to the federal judge in Fort Smith. Folks may attend if they're so inclined," barked the Marshall, spitting a long string of tobacco juice into a pile of hay.

"Ah, just as I suspected, sir." Judge Durand took a wide stance balancing himself on his walking stick and careful to avoid soiling his polished boots on horseshit. "Well I have come here to tell you that I am prepared to do you the service, which I'm sure you will appreciate, of saving you the inconvenience of sitting in a saloon full of the local rabble by informing you that this hearing is moot..."

"What the hell is moot? Moot who?" asked Dan Barkin.

Judge Durand smiled. "Meaning it is no longer necessary, if you will sir, and that you may be unfettered with this matter and on to more pressing affairs I'm sure, once your horse is able bodied."

"What the hell you talking about, mister?" asked Barkin as he again spit into the hay.

"What I am talking about, Marshall, is the futility in performing the same legal proceedings twice as it was I, an official magistrate in my own right, who witnessed and approved the death certificate that Doctor Rushman prepared."

The sheriff stood to his full six feet one inch height and looked squarely at the haughty figure posing in front of him with a ivory handled walking stick and gray kidskin gloves.

"Well what you're telling me ain't really that handy because if my memory serves me right, wasn't it you who allegedly shot and killed the man in question?"

"That I do not deny, sir. I am a man of honor and I was protecting my standing as a gentlemen. Surely, being a man of the law, you can appreciate the guiltlessness of my actions."

"This is the goddamndest thing I ever heard of," roared the Marshall. "Here is the man who pulled the trigger of the murder weapon telling me, the federal marshal of the territory, that there's no need for a hearing. That's a hell of a notion you got there mister - I'll have to tell that one to Hanging Judge Parker back at Fort Smith. That'll surely crack 'em up something awful," he guffawed.

The Judge visibly stiffened: "Marshall, I remind you that I am a recognized judge in the noble state of Louisiana."

This time the sheriff spit his tobacco close to Durand's gleaming boots and patted his horse's rump. "And might I remind you that I've already one horse's ass next to me here and I don't need another one wasting my time, talking such nonsense. I'll see you at the hearing, *Mister* Durand."

Durand stood there in stony silence for a moment, his face turning red and his gloved hand tightly gripping the ivory handle of his walking stick. For his part, Barkin was almost hoping he'd strike him with that damn stick so he could just break this damn fool's jaw and be done with it. But finally Durand said not a word and just turned and walked away, not being the kind of man to risk rolling around a stable floor in a messy bout of fisticuffs.

During the hearing Petit Jean and his family sat in the same saloon where his father had been shot; mere feet from where John O'Keefe had lay dying. A dark bloodstain could still be made out under the sawdust on the rough wooden planked floor. Marshall Barkin wasted no time in calling the hearing to order at the specified time and briskly got on with the business of the day. Doc Rushman read his death certificate and then Durand, dressed in his finest pearl gray suit, took an oath and gave his own twisted version of the events of that afternoon: that John O'Keefe, losing badly at cards, had quit the table after accusing the Judge of cheating and suddenly drew his gun. The Judge said he had no other option but to respond in kind and had shot John O'Keefe in a fair fight. Of course, Carpis backed up his story and no other witnesses came forward to contradict their testimony.

Then Durand said, "I smelled whiskey on the man's breath when I sat down at the gaming table and I surmise he was intoxicated or he would never have offended an experienced duelist such as myself. For the sake of the man's bereaved family I truly regret this incident but a man cannot allow his honor to be tramped in the mud by every *pig farmer* who drunkenly stumbles into town."

At these words Petit Jean rose to his feet. The boy looked at his mother, tears rolling down Rose O'Keefe's cheeks. He stared at Durand and clenched his teeth so hard he thought they might shatter to pieces in his mouth.

"Marshall, can I say something?" he asked in a shaky voice, catching Dan Barkin by surprise and causing the twenty or so farmers, cowboys and miners gathered in the room to hush. Doc Rushman, who sat next to the Marshall, whispered that this was John O'Keefe's boy who was there during the shooting but as a minor was certainly too young to

21

be an official witness for the inquiry.

The sheriff nodded to the boy, "Well...if you got something to say, son, you best get on with it."

"My pa was not drunk and he took but two drinks of whiskey in this here saloon that day, so help me God. If you're here looking for the truth sir, well...the truth is he was cheated by those two men standing here today in this here room and than murdered in cold blood as sure as I'm sitting here - and they both knows it and that's the truth, so help me God...again." While he spoke Petit Jean pointed a shaking finger at Durand and the stinking Carpis who cowered by the judge's side looking guilty as sin. Those attending the hearing in the saloon erupted noisily but Durand immediately rose to his feet and loudly stomped his walking stick three times on the rough planked floor and shrieked out over the noise.

"Marshall, I can sympathize with the grief of this destitute pitiful family here but even that does not excuse such defamation of character by this little...mongrel. I demand that you arrest this boy on the serious charge of false accusation and let him experience the inside of a dark jail cell for a few lonesome nights as a preventative measure to his insolence while I consider my course of action, so that he might not follow in the footsteps of his sorry father."

Dan Barkin, a lawman already some ten years, had seen the territory of his jurisdiction grow during that time to attain some semblance of civilized law and order. Once wide-open spaces were quickly being dotted with settlements. For twenty years, outlaws, murderers and bank robbers had crossed over from Missouri and Kansas to find refuge among the *Civilized Nations* as long as they violated no tribal statutes and more often than not it had been his job to go in alone, negotiate with the Indian chiefs and bring the criminals back to Fort Smith to face justice. That was the kind of work he had signed on to this job for, not this damn reading aloud from the Federal Statute Book lying in front of him, worded in such a way that he could barely understand it himself.

Since the Civil War's end, the Oklahoma border was filling up with farmers and ranchers - even banks and saloons, much of the land already controlled by anonymous livestock companies incorporated back east, and a Marshall's once freewheeling job had become inundated with three days worth of paperwork for every outlaw he managed to catch up with. Nowadays, the only time he got a sense of who he was anymore was when he was riding out on the prairie alone without politicians or citizens' groups telling him how he ought to do his job.

Dan Barkin was getting on towards the end of his rope here in Vendee and was itching to put this useless hearing behind him; knowing it to be just a wasted formality in the absence of a real judge for this part of the country. Although he had shot ten men dead in the streets, saloons and hills of the territory and hauled more than he cared to remember to end their days standing on a wobbly plank with a hangman's noose around their neck, begging for mercy from their maker, he knew that without any eyewitnesses to the dispute, he would be forced to take Judge Durand at his word with Carpis as his witness. There was little else he could do - even if he was so disposed to do so - to get to the bottom of things on a one-day visit to the shaggy town of Vendee.

Dan Barkin didn't much care for Durand's high-toned airs but he knew that arrogance couldn't be the measure of whether a man was guilty of murder. At the same time he surely didn't like the pitiful sight of this pretty young widow and her two children sitting there before him with their teary, red eyes as big as saucers, looking toward him alone, like he was President Grant, to make sense out of this killing which had blown a family's hopes of a happy life together to kingdom come.

"Nobody is going to put this boy in jail as long as I'm wearing a badge in this territory. This is a goddamn public hearing and anybody I care to call on can speak his mind freely and plainly with no fear of any reprisal," said Barkin to Durand. "And you Mister Durand, you sit down until I call on you again."

Durand stood stiffly for a moment and then took the nearest chair. Carpis stood there just a few feet away from the Marshall looking confused and grunting.

"And tell your man Carpis to either take a bath or wait outside this saloon."

The saloon erupted in laughter as Carpis scampered out of the room.

"Hush up!" barked the Marshall. The he turned to the boy.

"Son, how much money had your daddy sold his pigs for before entering this here saloon that afternoon?"

"Sir, we brought six pigs into town and I should know because I sat

24

in the back of the wagon with those smelly hogs pissing all over me..."
Petit Jean had not meant to be funny but again all in the barroom broke
into laughter.

"Quiet down back there," said the sheriff. "Son, you were saying?"

"Yes sir, he sold all six pigs to Mr. Cooks round back at the
stockyards for thirty dollars a piece. My pa said he should have gotten
more but that Cooks was a cheap son of a..."

Again the room broke out laughing and a red-faced Mr. Cooks, who
ran the local stockyards for a large consortium that shipped beef and pork
back east, slumped down in his chair.

"And your Pa lost all that money at this here table, son?"

"Yes he did, sir. Of course, he was winning some when he was
playing with them cowboys and Doc Rushman, and he was feeling pretty
pleased with himself about that, but once Judge Durand and that Carpis
sat down he was wiped out pretty darn quick and that's when he
suspected that there was some trickery going on."

"So he lost all of..." the sheriff counted on his fingers. "That would
be one hundred eighty dollars?"

"Yes sir, I reckon that's it..." The boy looked down at the floor. "Not
counting that he lost his life as well."

Barkin sat brooding in his chair, looking at the boy. He had better
things to do than to be presiding over this makeshift hearing on a spring
afternoon, the saloon stinking of spilled whiskey and the sweat of the
working cowmen and miners gathered in the back. There was but one

25

woman in the whole place, Rose O'Keefe. Dan Barkin had seen plenty of widows like her before: coming out to the prairie young and pretty and hopeful with an ambitious husband bound and determined to strike it rich through farming or cattle but who too often ended his days stretched out under a lonesome pile of rocks in back of a clapboard church, his dreams done in by Indians or rustlers or just plain weariness and sickness. And soon all the youth and hope is drained from a young widow's eyes and her life becomes a daily struggle just getting her family through each winter alive until she finally finds her own place under another heap of rocks in some in some windswept church cemetery. These were the real heroes of the frontier, thought Dan Barkin, not tin badge lawmen such as himself or strike it rich miners, but these prairie wives whose exhausting lives were all worked out in advance, unbeknownst to them, the moment they set a foot into that long covered wagon back east, heading west toward their destiny which so often lay so far from their dreams.

Dan Barkin took out his gun and pounded the butt end on the table to quiet the room. "This here's what I decide in the case of the shooting of John O'Keefe. You..." he pointed to Durand who immediately stood rigidly at attention, "You are to pay this women one hundred eighty dollars before leaving this room. And as there be no other witnesses to this here incident I reckon I'll have to declare that John O'Keefe was shot in self-defense."

Durand's shrill voice screamed in protest, "Marshall, I object to this mimicry of justice as a citizen of this territory and as a judge of the state of Louisiana. There are no legal grounds for me paying this women one red cent. Her husband lost his...his pig money, in a fair game of chance...."

Dan Barkin slammed the table hard with his gun butt and slowly stood up himself. The room hushed. "Here's the deal," he said gruffly, his eyes narrowing on Judge Durand. "Either you pay this poor widow here the one hundred eighty dollars as I have ordered you to by the time I ride out of town this evening or I will take you - and your stinking hired man as well – along with me and you'll both be put in a cell back in Fort Smith, Arkansas, to face Judge Parker when he comes around next month." The sheriff slammed the butt end of his revolver hard again on the table. "And this here ain't Louisiana by a long shot, mister."

The saloon was still and all eyes were on Durand now, but none more steadily than the Marshall's own, whose gun was now resting under his own hand on the table in front of him. A few tense moments passed before Durand finally walked the few steps separating him from the O'Keefe family. He stood just inches in front of the boy and Petit Jean could smell the sickly sweet odor of the Judge's hair tonic and cologne.

"I will give this women the one hundred eighty dollars as so ordered, Marshall, but I say to everyone in this room that I have broken no law of this territory and any ill doing brought upon this poor women and her family was brought down upon them by her own irresponsible drunkard of a husband." He counted out some bills and coins and dropped the money at Petit Jean's feet. The boy bent down and picked it up and handed it gently up to his mother. And than he stood up as full sized as he could muster, coming just under Durand's chin.

"Murderer," he said in a voice louder than a whisper but clear enough for the whole room to hear. Durand raised his walking stick over his head.

"Don't!" said Barkin holding his gun in his hand.

Durand's eyes went wide as if in a trance and then he slowly lowered his walking stick, smiled at Rose O'Keefe, and bowed to the courtroom before walking out of the saloon.

"Rebel son of a…," began Marshall Dan Barkin but then he stopped himself. "This hearings over," he said as he put his pistol somewhat reluctantly back into his holster

Chapter 3

That sorrowful evening when Petit Jean, his ma and his little sister Antoinette drove back home from Vendee following the hearing, nearly silent in their creaking wagon, there was but one faint star in the sky and no moon at all. As he sat in the darkness, Petit Jean tried to make himself believe in a miracle; that when they arrived home he would open his eyes and awaken from this nightmare to find his pa come running and laughing out of the barn like always, his big red Irish face smiling at them as he ran his hands through his son's blond hair. But as they drove up the dark road that approached their farm there was only the sound of the wagon wheels rolling on the dirt road and the forlorn sight of the solemn and dark house there to greet them. It was as if they were all alone in this sad universe and Petit Jean figured that God just didn't give a damn about him and his family anymore and for some reason unbeknownst to the boy He had forsaken them all. In the desolation of his broken young heart he tried to accept that his beloved father was gone out of his life forever.

That bleak night, the three of them slept in the same bed together: Petit Jean, his sister Antoinette and his mother Rose O'Keefe, sometimes one or all of them crying while trying hard to reassure each other that everything was going to be alright, that it would somehow have to be alright. Then suddenly, in the dark of the moonless night his ma woke up, got up from the bed and walked right out of the house in her bare feet with a hastily lit lantern, dressed only in her bed clothes in the chill of the spring night air. Swinging up the heavy wooden door on the ground next to the barn, she stepped down into their cyclone cellar and began to make a rip-roaring mess of anything and everything she could lay her hands on: flinging open trunks and baskets and throwing piles of letters and books every which way.

Petit Jean had followed his mother to the steps of the cellar.

"Mama, what you are looking for in the middle of the night?" he yelled down.

"Walt Whitman," his mother replied.

For as long as Petit Jean could remember, the sacred name of Walt Whitman had been spoken by his mother on so many different occasions and with such a warm and tender familiarity that the boy had come to regard the barely celebrated poet as just one more of his remote and distant kin; some prominent member of his ma's faraway family like his grandpa and namesake big Jean the Frenchman who still lived back east off Long Island sound, far, far from the dusty prairies of the Old Oklahoma border.

Rose O'Keefe would often say that she could still remember Walt Whitman sitting by the smoky fireplace in her own Papa's tavern for hours upon hours, stroking his chin while composing verse after verse of his ever changing "Leaves Of Grass." She distinctly remembered his otherworldly expression changing in intensity from fear to joy to rapture and tears as the words took flight from his mind and he impatiently

30

scratched them down onto his inky notebooks. She imagined it was her own papa's tasty French cooking which drew the poet back to the tavern when he was rambling on Long Island's north shore but also figured it was the joyful cries of all the town's children who played just outside. Sometimes during late afternoons when the children were out from school and while most other men were still hard at work, Walt Whitman would play hoops with the youngsters of the town, laughing and screaming with the lot of them, his own eyes sparkling with the same magical sense of childish wonder. Of course, explained Rose O'Keefe, this was before the terrible Civil War when Whitman went off to help tend to the dead and dying as a male nurse in the military hospitals around Washington DC. Folks said that when he returned north he was a profoundly changed man with a new look of sorrow around his eyes. And yet he was still fiercely determined to celebrate himself and the mysteries of the universe itself in his writing, while at the same time trying to come to terms with a nation gone mad on a feast of brotherly blood.

Rose O'Keefe told her own children the story of how she first met Walt Whitman when she was just a child herself, barely even in her teens, and already struggling to clear dirty dishes off the heavy oaken tables in her papa's crowded tavern in Huntington Harbor on the north shore of Long Island. Whitman's appearances at the tavern were an exciting event for the small town. Although he was living in Brooklyn and toiling as editor in chief of *The Brooklyn Star* when the summer weather turned balmy he saw no problem in letting the newspaper manage on its own for days at a time - much to the annoyance of the tabloid's owners - while he trekked out to his beloved Long Island. He might journey to the very tips of the twin forked eastern end to Greenpoint on the north where ferries crossed the sound to Rhode Island or Montauk with its fabled lighthouse on the longer southern fork but he always stopped to pay a call at Huntington, the region of his birth.

Rose recollected how she once tried to take an empty soup bowl off of Walt Whitman's table when suddenly he gently seized her wrist and stopped her in the middle of her chores, asking if he might speak to her for a moment before she continued. He was a tall angular man, clean-shaven at this time, and prone to wearing the open necked shirts of the dockworkers back in Brooklyn whom he counted among his truest companions.

"Do you know you live on *Paumanok* my pretty young thing?"

She was shy to speak to him, but as her father had told her he was a celebrated journalist and must be treated with utmost respect whenever he came by the tavern, she felt obliged to respond in some way or another.

"Why...I thought this was Huntington, sir?" she replied softly.

"Well that it is, my dearie. But in this universe there are countless ways to refer to a thing or a place or a piece of land and you must know that long before we inhabited these plains it was the walkway of the Delaware Indians, who came out here to hunt and to fish."

"There ain't no Indians here now, I hope," she said frightened; the recent Sioux massacre of Minnesota settlers was still in the news.

"No, not too many left in these parts, I suppose. Guess we pushed them all out west or worse. But in the ancient tongue of the Delaware Indians they called this place, this Long Island *Paumanok* – because it means it was shaped like a fish. Now what do you think about that my sweetie?"

The little girl had eyed him warily for it was rare that an adult would speak to her in such a learned way.

"I don't think anything about that, sir," she said. "But I guess I better get these dishes into my papa's kitchen before he comes out here and hollers at me."

Whitman laughed. "Oh they'll be plenty of time for working I'm afraid," he said, his eyes sparkling. "You're a good little girl my fancy, but before you go, allow me to give you something to remember me and yourself by." He thought for a moment and then scribbled something on the sheath of paper in front of him, ripped off his few lines of writing, folded it and handed it to the young girl.

"Now can you promise me something?"

"Depends what it is. My papa says I shouldn't make promises if I don't aim to keep them."

"Don't you worry, my fancy. This is an easy one. I want you to take this bit of verse I wrote for you and to hide it amongst your most cherished things. Do you think you can do that for me?"

"I reckon I could."

"Put it among your silk bows and pearl buttons and promise me to

33

never show it to anybody until you're all grown up someday, remembering when you were but a precious young girl, living on Paumanok and talking to me, Walt Whitman."

Then he asked her to bring him a heaping plate of the baby bluefish that teemed and swirled and broke water in the nearby harbor come late summer every year and that her papa fried to perfection in oil and butter.

Sundays, after Catholic mass, her papa would walk with her through the long dune grasses and on to the beach and gaze out over choppy Long Island Sound toward the hazy Connecticut shoreline. Big Jean often spoke of how badly he missed the Arcadian mountains up in Canada where he grew up and how he was more then fed up with the flatness of Long Island and the pious demeanor of his puritan Anglo-Saxon neighbors. But still he said he would never return north again to live in French speaking Canada, for he blamed the arctic winds for the deadly chill that had taken his own young bride Annabel from him soon after Rose was born. Following his wife's death, Big Jean had worked his way down through New England with his baby daughter in tow, finally ferrying across the sound to Long Island where he had found home and livelihood in the quaint whaling harbor of Huntington. It was a place where ship's captains stoically added boxlike "widow's walks" to top off their impressive houses and help lonely wives pass the long months of a whaling ship's voyage and a far away husband, anxious eyes scanning the horizon each evening hoping to sight a schooner already weeks late to home and safe port.

Huntington Harbor was a quiet still-water port off Long Island

Sound where ships would stock up on supplies before heading back out to the North Atlantic, often for months at a time, chasing sperm whale and filling their holds with oil and blubber. Petit Jean's mother had passed an idyllic and carefree childhood there, playing on the pebble strewn beaches with her friends and trekking through the muddy marshes at low tide, with her papa in his high oil-slicked boots gathering oysters and clams while he set crab traps. Clenching a curved pipe under his droopy moustache, Big Jean would sing her the old world songs of his own youth always speaking to her in French as the sea wind whooshed in her hears and brought a taste of salt to her mouth. And when Petit Jean was a baby, his ma did the same with him, singing soft French lullabies and often chattering away to the pigs in French as well. The pigs, oddly enough, always seemed to react faster to her calls sung out in a shrill French compared to those delivered in the clipped English of her husband.

Rose O'Keefe adored her children and had loved her husband dearly but never the dusty, arid land of the Oklahoma border country where John O'Keefe staked his claim. When she was a girl her dreams were of marrying a whaling ship's captain and sailing to all the exotic ports of the seven seas at his side. But from the evening the young Private John O'Keefe strolled into her father's tavern, still dressed in his union blues, and saw her emerge from the swinging kitchen doors, a beautiful strawberry blond girl in full bloom at eighteen years old, with a milkmaid's rosy cheeks and a relaxed friendly way about her, those dreams of hers, like those of so many other women, were replaced by the dreams of their

35

husband.

John O'Keefe had sat entranced as he watched her whisk in and out of the kitchen and around the tavern, her arms full of steaming hot bowls of ham and lentil soup. He was struck dumb by her freshness, her vitality, and when once she bent low next to him to retrieve a fallen spoon and he caught a whiff of the flowery fragrance of her hair, he thought he might faint dead away then and there. This young waitress who he only knew as *Rose* became as passionate a cause for him to dedicate his life to as that of saving the Union itself.

After hours of silently admiring her he finally got up the nerve to try to speak to her.

"Could I bother you for another ale, Rose?" he asked.

"And what do you think I'm here for? It's no bother - I'll bring it right to you soldier. And how did you know my name was Rose, might I ask."

"Why, I heard your father calling you from the kitchen. Although, if I might say so, the name doesn't suit you in my opinion.

"And why be that soldier?"

"Because I have never seen a rose as pretty as you."

Rose blushed all the way to the kitchen and when her father asked her what was wrong she said something about carrying the hot soup too close to her face. Soon John O'Keefe was ordering drinks for most of the men of his company, taking any excuse to talk to her and Rose smiled politely when she served him and tried not to show any particular notice or interest in him although that was difficult for even she sensed there was something different about him. His spirit still seemed so vibrant, unlike so many of the other broken union veterans who were making their way home back north, back from the killing fields of Virginia and Georgia; some missing arms or legs and all still dressed in their dark blue uniforms and rakish infantry caps. The returning troops drank ale and beer, played cards and argued about the war, the battles, the Union's military strategy and, of course, the lingering conspiracy theories behind Abe Lincoln's murder; many still convinced there existed a giant and still powerful rebel army, waiting just across the border in northern Mexico, biding its time for a ferocious rear attack on the union's western territories.

John O'Keefe had miraculously come out of the brutal fighting unscathed, and he quickly replaced all the weight lost in a Confederate prison camp thanks to Jean Wagram's cooking and was back to his usual stocky build. With his tightly waved red hair and broad, clean shaven freckled face, he was more appealing to Rose than most of the soldiers she served and had come to answer his freely offered smile with a shy curtsey of her own, unsuspecting of how smitten he actually was with her. When the tavern closed and John O'Keefe would go back to his barracks he prayed that all he wanted in this world was for Rose to return his love in kind and be the mother of his yet unborn children.

Ironically, his prayers were truly answered and Rose Wagram would be John O'Keefe's one and only true love for what was left of his too short life. Together, they would cross the frontier and take a piece of the country he had fought for as their own. Like any ambitious young man, fears about his own mortality had not yet even entered into John O'Keefe's psyche. He never even harbored the harrowing thought that his own aspirations of conquering the frontier and living a settler's life with his family were to be cut short; that after crossing half of the wide American continent with his pretty young bride, he would leave her a grieving widow, unable to care for his two children and spiritually ruined while still in the prime of her life.

While his regiment moved on up to Boston, John O'Keefe managed to get himself discharged right there on Long Island and after a year of steady courting, he eventually broke down Rose's resistance (as well as that of her burly papa, Jean) and one bright summer day with the cherry blossoms trees bursting pink, he married her in a Catholic ceremony held in the small sailor's chapel overlooking Long Island Sound. Jean Wagram shed a tear and swore to all who cared to listen that he knew in his heart that he would never see his little girl again, that this wild Irishman John O'Keefe would take her far, far away from him.

And a short time afterward John O'Keefe did exactly that when he and Rose Wagram O'Keefe loading all their earthly possessions into a long Conestoga wagon bound for St. Louis to join a wagon train that would bring them even further west - all the way to the border of the Indian Territory - Old Oklahoma. The bubbling excitement of an eighteen year old girl, never having set foot off Long Island before and about to set out on a journey across the American continent, far overshadowed any fear or trepidation on her part and she merrily kissed her papa once on each cheek goodbye, never imagining it would be forever.

The expedition itself was arduous but uneventful; she and John O'Keefe spent long days hiking behind their wagon to save the lumbering oxen's energy as they crossed the plains in sizzling summer heat, miles stretching endlessly before them. Rose was disappointed to see but one shabby group of Indians, come to trade furs for food, tobacco or better whiskey when the wagon train camped outside St. Louis. The memory of their drawn, silent faces when they were turned away by the muleskinners who ran the outfit haunted her for some nights.

"You can't fight progress," consoled her husband.

They settled just outside the border of the unopened Indian Territory where the so-called five civilized tribes of Cherokee, Chickasaw, Choctaw, Creek and Seminole had been forcefully moved by the less then civilized U.S. government in the twenty five years between 1815 and 1840. The location of their land was advantageous for the servicing of provisions to the long cattle drives up from Texas to the railhead in Wichita, Kansas. There was even a windy scrap of a town nearby - Vendee - and John O'Keefe built a simple house of mud and timber and staked his modest but well placed farm just far enough outside town to keep his privacy intact and the road to Vendee brief. Within three years Rose delivered two healthy babies, first the boy, Jean, named after her own father, and than Antoinette, named after the doomed French queen of Louis XVI.

Theirs was a hardscrabble existence of farming, raising pigs and cows, fighting the dust storms of summer and the blizzards of a long winter, and always hoping but rarely able to come out with something extra to put them a little ahead for the next year, a routine none too different from that of most other settlers. But all in all they were happy and content and found brief and treasured moments to relax from the work of the farm. While nursing her two babies, Rose would feed them by the open hearth fire and recite passages from Walt Whitman's *Leaves of Grass*, telling her boy - who from birth was called "Petit" Jean - that she never could figure how Walt Whitman could just stare into the great fireplace of her father's tavern for hours at a time, blocking out the drunken laughter and loud talk of the sailors and the cooking smells of the smoky kitchen around him, all the while composing such glorious verse. She often promised to find that precious piece of paper on which Whitman had written down a little poem just for her when she was still a strawberry blond little girl of ten years old and read it aloud to the family over dinner. But she never did.

"When I have a few spare minutes that is!" she added, Free time, like milk or money, being a quantity never in sufficient supply on their farm.

"Of course," Rose would joke, as she spread slop in the pig pen or lugged the milking stool under a kicking cow, "With enough practice these hogs might soon be able to feed themselves, eventually sitting at the dinner table with the rest of us and one morning I might just find that the cows had delivered their milk right to the front door for a change. Well, then I'd have plenty of time for such niceties as poetry."

"Oh *Mon Dieu au paradis!*" she'd exclaim, wiping the sweat from her brow and looking down at her reddened, roughhewn hands, "If I'd just known what this Irishman - *ce fou* John O'Keefe! - had in mind for me, I might never have left my papa's side. Now I can hardly tell you how I ache for just one sunny summer day to walk on a windy beach in the late afternoon, breathing in that delicious sea air, without the smell of the pigs in my nose and the scorched taste of this prairie in my mouth. Voila! You see what love can do to a young girl."

But Rose O'Keefe never did feel the wet sand under her feet again nor hear the squawking sea gulls.

Chapter 4

Much to the objections of her husband, Rose had insisted upon bringing a hefty trunk full of books and childhood mementos out west with her. John O'Keefe thought it a waste of what little space there was in the covered wagon that also had to serve as kitchen and sleeping quarters during the long journey. And in fact, many of those things like the dolls and porcelain, which once had seemed so precious to young Rose, were now covered with a greenish tint of mildew and gathering dust in the cold dirt cellar next to the farmhouse, picking up the earthy smell of the growing mound of sweet potatoes lying next to them. Petit Jean himself had spent many hours in that damp cellar, helping his ma seal and label jars of preserved fruits and vegetables and stacking them in a corner, although he couldn't recall his ma looking through any of those stacked books when they'd been down there together.

But on that night after they returned home from the hearing in Vendee she ripped through those books like a wild banshee, getting down to her knees and praying that she would only find what she was looking for, some words the poet had written for only her. Please God, she prayed, let it be there so that she might find some answers, some solace for her terrible pain and fear that her own life, like her husband's, would be soon lost, gone, blown away on this terrible expanse of prairie and dust. Then, while scourging through the cellar Rose O'Keefe came across a well hidden bottle of her husband's Irish whiskey, presumably saved for some special occasion - Christmas or a birth - and as she held the bottle in her trembling hands she saw the image of her husband's face in the way the facets of the brown glass reflected the oil lamp she carried and as the whiskey splashed inside the bottle she held it on high and gulped it down with the ardor of a nursing baby. It was surely the first hard liquor she had ever tasted in her life and the warmth of the alcohol spread from her stomach to the tips of her fingers and her face began to sting and pulsate as she felt first flushed and nearly overcome with the sensation, afraid she might vomit and pass out all at once. When the liquor finally settled, she felt a heavy weight take her by the shoulders and her knees collapsed causing her to fall to the cold clay floor and she was sure that in some minutes she would be as dead as her husband, imagining the hands of God himself pushing her further down and burying her here in the cold clay earth.

But soon the warmth of the whisky overcame the dampness of the floor and she settled into that soothing intoxicating hum that held sway over her, flowing like a current down her spine. And when that first rush of the liquor passed, and she realized that she was not dead and apparently wasn't going to die momentarily, she again brought the bottle to her mouth and kept pulling it in until it was half empty, ignoring the anguished cries of Petit Jean and young Antoinette who sat huddled in a blanket at the top of the cellar stairs, listening anxiously to their ma wailing and moaning and cursing her own dead husband's name; going on and on like a deranged soul in both English and French.

43

"John O'Keefe you bastard! To die like that and to leave me here with your children in this God forsaken place. Tell me, John, what am I to do now? Who can tell me what I am to do now! *Tu es un salaud - un vrai salaud!*" After hours of this shrieking when her voice was as hoarse as a witch she began pounding her fists and than her head into the clay earth of the walls of the cellar until finally, mercifully, she fell to the mossy ground unconscious.

In a deep sleep Rose O'Keefe continued to moan throughout the night and then when dawn came and the sun rose up from the direction of Missouri, the cellar turned quiet. The two children had sat at the cellar doors wide eyed and nearly paralyzed with fear all night long and they listened for a long time before creeping down the wooden stairs to find their mother lying in a pile of books, loose papers and sweet potatoes, sound asleep with the sweet, sickly smell of whiskey creeping out of her every pore. In her open hand lay a crumpled piece of paper, which Petit Jean carefully stuck in his long johns before going to the barn, fetching a hemp rope and hitching it around his mother's waist. Then he went up the cellar stairs, leaned against the barn and started pulling and tugging that rope with all his might while Antoinette yelled in her mama's ear: "Stand up mama! Walk mama!" and somehow they managed to haul Rose up the steps like a roped cow. With a tremendous effort each child draped one of her arms over their small shoulder and walked her back to the farmhouse, finally laying her down on her own bed. Rose was still covered with the soot and dirt of the cellar and smelling rank and musky from lying on the

44

wet, mud floor all night long. The tiny Antoinette lay down next to her mama and tried to comfort her, stroking her tangled hair, but when Rose O'Keefe became conscious enough to recognize her daughter lying beside her, she began crying and moaning and calling for Petit Jean's pa all over again.

The children had no breakfast and when it looked like their ma might never regain her senses, Petit Jean told his sister to wait with her and make sure she didn't go back down into that cellar while he took the mule to ride to the Filloux place some five miles north. The boy could just as easily have rode back to Vendee but his pride wouldn't allow that, to go back into that damned town and shamefacedly tell all those people who had watched Judge Durand throw his money at her feet while accusing his father of being a drunkard, that his own mother was now lying drunk and sick and deranged back at their farm. No, he swore to himself, he would never do that no matter what happened.

John O'Keefe had enjoyed brief but friendly contact with Edward Filloux, a neighboring farmer, some few times a year trading crops and livestock or helping to haul a tree stump or raise a barn roof in spite of the fact that ol' man Filloux was a Mississippian and John O'Keefe a veteran of Abe Lincoln's army. But when ol' man Filloux walked out of his barn after hearing the steady hoof beats of Petit Jean's mule and spotted the boy trotting up the path to his farm he was even more welcoming than usual. Word had quickly spread from the Vendee saloon throughout the territory of how the hot-headed Irishman John O'Keefe

45

had drawn his gun right in front of his own boy and after a short firefight had been left bleeding and dying, his head cradled in his son's arms. But Edward Filloux knew John O'Keefe to be a fair man and not nearly so willful that he would be raring to shoot it out like so many of the young cowboys who rode through town, down from Dodge City or up from Fort Worth, who within no time at all were drunk and brawling and firing pistols into the sky. No, he imagined that John O'Keefe had fallen prey to any one of a number of snares awaiting an honest man who falls into a card game with the wrong sort, the west seeming to attract in equal proportion as many thieves and murderers as honest farmers and ranchers.

Filloux was a tall, lanky man whose ironic resemblance to the abolitionist martyr John Brown with his long gray beard and dour expression had pushed him to fight harder than most of the Confederate troops at the battle of Vicksburg. He watered Petit Jean's mule while the boy tried as best he could to explain his ma's troubles, kicking his foot in the dirt, never daring to look Filloux in the eye. Filloux spoke softly to the boy and walked him into his farmhouse where his wife, a small woman who rarely spoke and always wore a bonnet (by all accounts to cover an ugly scar from a botched Shawnee scalping when she was a child in Kentucky) fixed up some provisions - bread and smoked meats - for him to take on home.

"Just let your ma be for a few days, put a damp rag on her forehead and don't pay too much attention to anything she might say, as she most likely won't remember much herself when she finally comes to her senses. Don't you and your little sister worry son, she'll be back to her old self in no time," he consoled Petit Jean, but the boy was not so convinced.

"I suspect that if you and your little sister there can just lay out some hay for the animals and try and milk them cows before sundown that your daddy's farm will run itself just fine for a day or so." He laid his hand on the boys shoulder. It was the first genuine affection the boy had received from a man since the last time his own father had put an arm around him and Petit Jean stood silent and fought hard to hold back the tears; just nodding his head up and down, his emotions suspended in space, flying and unwilling to land on his heart or to be seen by anybody else. He felt that as long as he kept nodding his head he would not start crying. It was a habit he would hold on to long into manhood.

"Just let your ma be son...she's grieving and a woman has a right to grieve for either husband or child as long as it might take her."

"Thank you sir, I appreciate your kindness. My pa always said you was a good man even if you was a rebel." Then Petit Jean looked down and thought maybe he said something he shouldn't have, but Edward Filloux smiled kindly and when Petit Jean offered to pay him for the watering and feeding of his mule, which was what his father always did, Filloux just shook his head "no" and gently told him he better get on home before sunset.

He did add one other thing as the boy was riding away: "Now you be sure to get your ma and sister down into that root cellar if you should see any spouts of dark rain and wind way off in the fields, you hear me boy?"

"Yes sir," said Petit Jean. Filloux had already lost most of one farm back in Mississippi to a killer cyclone two years before moving to Old Oklahoma and now had become a self-styled expert on the subject of tornadoes to anyone who would care to listen. Said he could smell them coming before any man could see one; in fact, he claimed they made his nose start to itch a good hour before the dark winds came into view.

"Nothing in God's almighty wrath is worse then a wind spout from hell," he told the boy. "You can believe that." But Petit Jean could imagine nothing worse in all of God's power and fury than his pa laying bleeding and dying and begging his tormentors to leave him to die in peace with his boy, and he wondered truly what kind of a mean-spirited and wrathful God would allow such misery to be brought to his poor family.

"And son," Filloux shouted again after the boy as his mule started to trot home, "Your pa was a decent and honest man ...even for a blue-coat. Don't let anybody tell you different." And he spit on the dusty ground and sniffed up wind for cyclones.

Petit Jean and Antoinette sat up with their mother for another terrible night, her being sicker than they ever remembered: cradling her head in her hands, saying that her poor heart was about to burst and praying that she might be taken then and there by death's hand like her husband John O'Keefe himself, and climb up to God's kingdom of Heaven. And then the next morning, as if nothing had happened, she got

48

up and made a pot of strong coffee in the same way she always had, clanking the heavy kettle onto the stove and throwing in a pinch of sweet, pungent chicory like Petit Jean's father had liked it and drinking two strong cupfuls. After washing herself with a bucket of cold, well water she went out to the smokehouse and brought back cured ham for breakfast. Petit Jean watched her movements closely, saying nothing but noting the sad lines grown under her dark eyes and the way the corners of her mouth now turned downward. Rose O'Keefe put the food on the table for breakfast and after the children sat down and began eating she finally spoke.

"Antoinette, I'm sorry to not have any fresh bread for you today as I know how fond you are of dipping it into your milk. But I promise you, *mon petit loupiot*, that I'll get some dark bread baking right away, in time for supper."

Antoinette didn't look up.

"Well then, how about you and I bake a sweet rhubarb and honey pie for dinner as well? Would that bring a smile to my baby's lips?"

At this the little girl couldn't help but smile but when Rose O'Keefe smiled back it came out a hard, straight line with no trace of joy. Then, after clearing the breakfast dishes, she went to work, feeding pigs, milking cows and tending the crops with a kerchief tied over her mouth and nose to block the dust.

For little Antoinette the promise of having sweet rhubarb pie with supper that evening was assurance enough that life was back to normal and she sang sweetly as she played with her raggedy doll spread out under the shade of the low elm tree in front of the farmhouse. But for Petit Jean, it was as clear as the new lines on his ma's face that nothing would ever be the same again, rhubarb pie or not. For just like his ma, these long days and nights of grieving had irrevocably changed him as well, even if he had no worry lines on his young face to show it. For in the thick of his ma's drunken anguish and in the dark of night he had slipped his Pa's derringer out from the top drawer of their huge French armoire, brought all the way out west from Long Island in that long wagon and down from Canada before that. He held the small pistol with its smooth nickel finish in his hand for some time, quietly stroking the barrel, before taking it out in the barn and up into the gallery where the alfalfa and oats were stored to dry. Carefully wrapping the pistol in an oilcloth he hid it in the V-joint of two large overhead beams. Then he stood up on the hay gallery under the roof of the barn, puffing out his boyish chest and raising himself to all his meager height. He held his eyes tightly shut and squeezed his fists firm and as the sizzling colors phosphoresced under his eyelids and his hands began to ache he began quietly talking to his pa somewhere up in heaven, where he supposed he might be by now, John O'Keefe never having done anything the boy was aware of that would have sent him the other way. The horses were stomping their hoofs and raising little piles of dust and slivers of moonlight slid through the cracks in the ceiling boards above him.

"So help me if there's a God above in this heavenly sky," the boy promised his pa. "Someday I will hold the barrel of this here Derringer - your own gun pa - right up against the temple of Judge Durand and blow his brains to kingdom come even if that means that as a mortal sinner myself I will be obliged to follow the judge down into the fiery pits of hell for eternity. I swear this to you pa with God as my witness."

And after he had said goodbye to his father as best he could and thanked him for bringing him into this world and the things he had taught him about men and farming and horses and pigs, he carefully wiped the tears from each of his eyes before heading back outside the cellar, joining his sister sitting vigil on his mother, waiting for her and the world to return to their old selves and not sure they ever would.

Of course, his Ma had insisted that everything would return to normal even though his pa was gone, and they would all be OK, but Petit Jean couldn't bring himself to believe her or to believe that she was even convinced herself. In fact, he wasn't so sure if she was ever telling the truth about anything anymore - including this strange character Walt Whitman for that matter - or that she even knew anymore in the stormy anguish of her bereaved mind the difference between what was real and what was just the elixir of her tortured imagination.

Come the next Sunday, Petit Jean, his Ma and little Antoinette took the wagon back into Vendee to attend Mass and after the service they put wild poppies on John O'Keefe's grave where it stood alone out back of the chapel under a small patch of stones and a whitewashed cross. He was alone in the graveyard because his ma said that nobody had really been

51

living in the damn town of Vendee long enough to die there, speaking of Catholics of course, except their own father.

"Of course, the trail west is dotted with the graves of old folks and babies who died on their way out here, and, as much as their kin might have wanted to lay them to rest in this, their place of final destination, they never made it. Kind of sad don't you think?"

She put her arms around her children and looked down at his grave, the town itself quiet as a tomb on that Sunday morning. "At least your pa made it out west," she said as the three of them stood motionless watching the pedals of the wild flowers blow out toward the prairie on the warm summer wind. "At least you could say that about him if nothing else. Amen."

Chapter 5

There were dozens of towns like Vendee all over the Kansas and Oklahoma border, dotted with feeble dwellings that had the appearance of drifting about the barren land propelled by prairie winds; most towns wrapped around a little white church, a stable, a dry goods store and, if they lasted long, a saloon, gambling parlor or whore house. Vendee, being far off the Chisholm Trail, had little hopes or expectations of becoming the next boomtown, a riotous places like Dodge City or Abilene, and if it's stubby main street had any distinction to it at all, it was the extravagance of hosting two small churches - one Catholic, one Baptist - at either end of the gutted ride-way. Such religious diversity being due to the marked differences in the beliefs of the original settlers which had included a fair number of practicing Catholics - Louisiana farmers with French names like Filloux or Murat or the large Bernardin family who eventually introduced silk farms to the west and ate rabbits at holidays – as well as protestants. And the name of Vendee was in homage to one of the founding fathers of the town whose ancestor's roots lay in the Vendee province of western France. His forebears had chosen to remain faithful to God and King during the bloody citizens revolt of 1789 and, like many loyalist families who had survived the post-revolutionary terror, had immigrated to the still French controlled territory of Louisiana, where loyalty to a king was not an issue as long as you were free and white. Many frontier towns hosted a unique ethnic or religious formation, be it the

Dutch towns of West Texas, the Bohemian sheepherders of Montana or Utah's fiercely independent Mormons. Vendee's French Catholic hegemony was just a natural evolution of one French family planting roots in the place and then another joining them and on and on like that through a few generations.

Among the many families that had quit France during the revolution was a certain aristocrat whose loyalty laid neither with King, God, nor country - François Xavier Du Rand - a large provincial landowner equally detested by his peasants and the court alike. And it was from this lineage that Abel Durand came, born with both a silver spoon and an abundance of hubris to fill it and feed himself from.

When Durand had volunteered in the Army of the Confederacy shortly after the outbreak of hostilities at Fort Sumter, South Carolina in 1861, it was with dreams of glory and conquest. But his aristocratic bearing did not sit well with fellow confederate officers and his request to join Jeb Stuart's Northern Virginia Cavalry was discretely turned down. Assigned to the demeaning duty of officer in charge of the guards at Andersonville prison just outside of Americus, Georgia, Durand felt humiliated by his position and so it was there where his conceit, vanity and resentment darkly blossomed into the crimson bloom of sadism. It was at Andersonville that he delighted in sending Union prisoners dying of Cholera or Diphtheria to dig water filled trenches in nearly freezing temperatures, where he appropriated any parcels of charitable food or medicine that made it through the battle lines for his own use, and where he often ordered the sick and dying to be bayoneted in their beds to "save them from suffering." And with a sickly grin stood by watching.

By all rights Durand should have been hung along side the condemned camp commandment Captain Henry Wirz when the Union Army liberated the camp at the war's end. A hasty military trial was convened in Washington some months after but he managed to save his own skin by agreeing to testify against Wirz and shift the blame to his superior officer. In the last ten months of the war 13,700 prisoners of war had died in the prison – nearly all enlisted Union privates; cannon fodder who had escaped the horrors of battle only to find themselves in the even worse hell hole of Andersonville. They lived in tents with no floors through freezing winters and at times the death rate was 150 per day, a numbing figure that Durand himself had no small part in maintaining.

Word of his fiendish activities at Andersonville and his traitorous testimony against Captain Wirz had spread through the defeated Confederacy and upon his return to Louisiana Durand was shocked to find himself ostracized by New Orleans society. A young lady from one of the better Baton Rouge families whom he had been seriously courting before the war quickly dismissed any possibility of marriage and a promised position on the city's court bench was abruptly revoked, no reasons given. For Abel Durand there was little choice but to forsake his former cushy life in the French quarter and immigrate west. Traveling with three trunks full of his precious wardrobe and the misfit guard he had befriended for his own fiendish purposes at Andersonville: Claude

Carpis, a demented and illiterate hillbilly from the Georgia Mountains whose family, it was claimed, still lived in trees.

Durand and Carpis had arrived in Vendee the same season Petit Jean was born on a kitchen table during his folk's first year on the frontier. A relatively easy birth, Doc Rushman came by a week later to check how the misses was doing to find Rose O'Keefe already back at work in the fields, the baby boy cradled in a shawl around her waist. Two years later Antoinette arrived, pushing John O'Keefe to work even harder on the farm just to feed and clothe his growing family. Soon, at Rose's suggestion, he began raising pigs and curing ham and bacon, a profitable sideline to growing wheat and corn, and selling the produce in town, always pleased with the tidy profit he cut for himself. But once, coming back from the monthly Saturday livestock market he barely spoke to his wife or children for hours, finally sitting down at the dinner table quiet and sullen, totally unlike his usually talkative self.

"What's wrong with you John?" Rose finally asked. "I hope you didn't take a drink in town that's caused you to act so curious this evening."

"Nothing...I just saw a ghost, that's all," he murmured.

The two children laughed and their father scolded them to hush, barking that this was not some Halloween phantom he had run into.

"One of the rebels who guarded us at Andersonville Prison," he said. "A real son of a..." He looked towards the children and abruptly stopped talking, it being impossible for him to describe the atrocities committed

56

there while looking at the bright and shiny faces of his two young children. John O'Keefe had entered the war almost a child himself; a naive young soldier of seventeen, hardly ready for the ways of the world not to mention the horrors of war. What he had witnessed in Andersonville, man at their most bestial and cruel, had scarred him deeply and it was loathsome to him to even talk about his prisoner of war experiences. And when he did talk about the war itself it was not as some hometown hero might gaily reenact the bloody battle of Vicksburg just to amuse the local children, it was with a seriousness of purpose that only punctuated the ravages both armies left in their wake and the awesome slaughter of good men's lives. John O'Keefe was not a vainglorious man, perhaps oversensitive to any slight or criticism and a little too proud of his own energy and abilities, but one could say that his only real vice was an occasional drink and game of cards and in truth he had gambled his Saturday bacon profits away on more than a few occasions but had also doubled his money on others. Most times he knew when to pull out of the game, usually breaking even or better.

But Petit Jean felt that his pa had gambled more than the money from selling six pigs in that Saturday game of poker with Judge Durand and Carpis; because just by sitting down at that table with two men he despised he had wagered his own poor life, bluffing on nothing but a big his pride and revenge and with little with to back it up. And in someway the boy felt that if his wooden six-shooter had only been real his pa would be alive today and he would have shot Durand and Carpis dead where they stood, no questions asked.

That the O'Keefe family had been set adrift like a ship who has lost its rudder in the midst of a hellish storm and that the strong winds of frontier life were more than likely to send them crashing into rocks of ruin without husband or father to steer the boat was evident to most folks in Vendee. Petit Jean had his own suspicions that his Ma was being short changed on the pigs and sides of bacon that she was selling in town and her newfound taste for liquor came back with a vengeance. Soon, it was getting on four days out of six (leaving one for Sunday mass) that she even tried to set her mind on running the farm like his pa had done and before long the livestock was suffering and crops were spoiling in the field. Right in the middle of a long working day Rose seemed to always find some excuse to go into town – a needed tool or seed - and inevitably she returned home a half a day later with an already half drunk bottle of whiskey and Petit Jean, being too young to really know what the hell to do about it, just sat by, listening to his ma cry and moan and vomit.

The only solitude he found was in the hay gallery of the barn, fingering his pa's pearl handled derringer and imagining the terrified look on Judge Durand's face when that bastard would wake up some night from a deep sleep to feel the cold steel pressing against his temple; the day when Petit Jean would whisper really close into his ear, *"This is from my Pa, from John O'Keefe, sir, the tortures of hell await you."* And then just when the judge looked him in the eye and started to rise with trembling lips and barely croaking out a scream before the bullet entered his brain, Petit Jean was sure he would finally feel that sense of justice, to use Durand's own words, *"...that this damned territory so badly needs."*

It was in late autumn, with winter close and dusk arriving earlier each evening that Father Bachet, the Vendee parish priest, came out to visit the family late one afternoon, riding an old gray mule with his long priestly cloak hanging nearly to the ground. Like most of the folks in his parish, Father Bachet was of French decent too, having done his Jesuit training up in Quebec and, not really wanting to spend his life converting heathen Iroquois, had gladly taken this assignment out in the prairie where the Catholic settlers who had built their church were anxious for a real priest to go with it. Father Bachet was handsome for a priest with a Celtic face and dark hair, his own parents having emigrated from the western coast of Brittany, but he was cynical for a man of God, full of doubts never voiced and not fit, spiritually nor morally, for such a profession. For the sake of appearances he kept a vestige of the Roman ritual he'd been trained in alive out here on the frontier where even candles could be difficult to come by.

Father Bachet happened to pick one of Petit Jean's ma's better days for his visit to the farm because on that particular day Rose was in the process of getting over a drunk rather then just getting into one.

The priest rode into the courtyard of the farm and Petit Jean came out of the barn to take his mule. He smiled at Petit Jean and patted young Antoinette on her red curls before going inside to the farmhouse to speak with Rose O'Keefe, who was lying in bed with a cloth on her forehead

59

and a bucket on the floor next to her. He stayed with her a long time while the children waited anxiously outside. After an hour or so Petit Jean peered in the window and saw the priest and his ma down on their knees praying. When the priest finally walked out of the house he was smiling and he again patted Antoinette as he passed her but when Petit Jean walked with him to the barn to fetch his old mule, Father Bachet told the boy to sit down on the milk stool for he had something of vital importance to tell him.

"You're going to be going back East for a while son," he said. "Maybe just for a year or two until things get sorted out here. Winter's coming and your ma is in no shape to run this farm and you're a fine boy and all but hardly yet a man who can look after all that needs to be done, and well, it will be best for everybody."

"And Antoinette?" Petit Jean could feel the panic rising from his belly. "Will she be coming with me?"

"No, she'll be staying with me at the church while your mother sells the farm and then she too will move into town as well. But don't you worry about them, son, they'll be alright, the good Lord will provide for your mother and sister, I can assure you."

"But where am I going?" Asked Petit Jean.

"You're going to stay with your late father's brother who lives on Manhattan Island and..."

"Uncle George?" interrupted Petit Jean. "My pa use to talk about him from time to time but I swear I never did set eyes on him myself. Why, he's a complete stranger to me. I can't go there. I want to stay here with my ma and my sister," he protested.

"Well, some months ago I took the liberty of writing to your Uncle George when I saw your ma's troubles growing worse and worse each day and he wrote me back saying that he'd be ready to take you in for a while if its the best thing for all concerned and if it would help your mother in particular. Apparently the man is a successful entrepreneur and has got some kind of a restaurant or tavern near the docks at the mouth of the Hudson River where the sailors come to eat. He's willing to take you in and provide work for you in his restaurant to cover your room and board, doing chores in the kitchen I suspect, until you're ready to come back west and help provide for your mother and sister."

Petit Jean looked into the recesses of the dark barn. "I guess I don't have much to say about it then, do I Father?"

"Son, I believe it is the will of God for your mother to get closer to the church and find some solace from her grief. She needs the hand of Jesus."

Petit Jean scuffed his foot in the dust. "Like I said, I guess I don't have much to say about it...it being the will of God and all."

"Trust me boy, it will be better for all concerned," smiled Father Bachet.

These most *concerned* turned out to be none other than Judge Abel Durand who was anxious for the boy to leave Vendee and who after buying the O'Keefe farm for maybe half of its real worth made a sizeable donation to Father Bachet's church. Astonishingly, he began to court the newly widowed Rose O'Keefe and set himself up as Antoinette's guardian and savior while in his most deranged and secret moments he deluded himself into believing that he was no different from any other recipient of the spoils of war.

Chapter 6

Perched above the entrance of George O'Keefe's restaurant in far off New York City hung a large ornately decorated sign proudly proclaiming "O'Keefe's Fine Food Emporium" in gold print and punctuated by green leafed clovers at either end to eliminate any doubts of the proprietors Emerald Isle origins. The gaudy billboard straddled the entire front of the neat Victorian brick townhouse, located just blocks from the bustling Hudson River docks at the end of Manhattan's 23rd Street, a major thoroughfare that circumvented the island from East River to Hudson River and was often congested with the daily traffic of horse drawn wagons bound for the piers. One would easily surmise that such a location would be perfect for an eatery feeding hungry droves of working men.

But in truth there was little nourishment, fine or otherwise, to be found behind the formidable green lacquered door adorned with a shining brass knocker figure of a tempting mermaid. Of course, if a well paying and steady client of *O'Keefe's Emporium* might find his hunger rising after a particularly strenuous evening, he could possibly persuade Hank the bartender into sending out for a few strings of beef jerky, washed down with the premium whiskey or ale always in ready supply at O'Keefe's, but for more substantial fare than that he would have to make his way out into the night in search of a real tavern.

Unseasoned visitors were often perplexed as to why the three round tables in the front room of O'Keefe's were perpetually set with full silverware and china service as games of Faro were dealt around dishes while not a crumb of honest food lay in sight. But if they became habitués of *O'Keefe's Emporium* they would soon appreciate that George O'Keefe was a man keenly aware of the cosmetic morals of the community that he served. Thus he shrewdly allowed the unlicensed and blatant gambling to go on in full sight of anyone who passed by the front windows to give the stuffy town matrons something to wag their tongues about.

As George O'Keefe's himself was fond of saying "If you think the way to a man's heart is through his stomach you're aiming too high!" and accordingly the real nourishment he offered was known far and wide by the moniker of "Georgie's Girls" by every sailor, merchant or politician who ever set foot through that fabled green door and lustfully browsed the "menu" of *O'Keefe's Emporium*: a bevy of seductive - or at least *available* - women opulently draped over the railing of the second floor balcony overlooking the bar, dressed in as little as might keep them warm and procurable for a few silver eagles seven days a week save Christmas and Easter, George being a good Catholic and all.

In all, George O'Keefe kept thirteen whores in his bordello, ranging from fat ol' Nell, a hardcore veteran at forty-five who reckoned to have logged more time on her back than on her feet, down to young freckled Kate - just off the boat from Belfast and whose trademark school girl dress of yellow bows set atop braided pigtails, appealed to the naughty, prurient interests of the day. George gave no mind to a girl's

64

background or color as long as she was willing to do the job called for, was of a decent age - say, over fifteen - and caused no trouble among the other ladies of the house. Aside from Nell and Kate, his *girls* also included two freed blacks both going by the name of Martha - Big Martha and Lil' Martha - who George had found huddled on the west side docks, come north to escape the terror of the newly formed nightriders of the Ku Klux Klan down in their native Tennessee. And there was also the stern and stout German Frau who went by no other name than "The Frau;" the aristocratic silky blond Edwina Biddle, whose monthly bouts of hysteria were easily subdued by a cooperative doctor's opiates; the three Chinese sisters: Me, Cum, and Qwik, obvious mischievous abstractions of their original Cantonese names. And there was also their youngest little sister, Qwing So, barely a teenager, of whom there lay a sacred understanding between George O'Keefe and the three older sisters that she was never to be recruited into the *trade* as all future hopes for the family rested with Qwing So whose duties in the house went no further than to sweep up cigar ashes by the bar and collect the soiled laundry and bedclothes each morning.

These nine (plus Qwing So) lived at the house and formed the cozy nucleus of George's de-facto family, along with Hank the bartender, an ex-army mate of George's, whose tastes ran the other way, towards the young lads, which enabled him to get on with his work without distraction. George also kept on four part-time girls: Hillary the pale Swede who also worked days out of her home in Brooklyn Heights servicing the swarms of workers who had begun to construct the elegant Brooklyn Bridge in 1870; bald Gertie who wore a raven black wig down to her waist and showed up most nights more inebriated then her customers; olive skinned Linetta, who lived with her nine brothers in the Italian ghetto on the lower east side and spoke not a work of English but could sing Verdi like an angel.

George allowed no pecking order among these women and a client might have his pick, all at the same price, with one notable exception: the incontestable star of the house, the delicious Georgia belle, Barbara Banner, who had broken more than a few hearts among Manhattan's gentry and whose private steady clientele kept her busy and off limits to the common sailors who came in drunk on Saturday nights. The honorable Mayor of New York himself was counted among Barbara Banner's more privileged clientele and he made his late night visits discretely from his shaded private carriage, journeying from his townhouse on Gramercy Park to enter discretely through the back door of Barbara Banner - both literally and figuratively.

Barbara lived in the finest room of the house, lavishly furnished by His Honor himself, who showered her with expensive gifts but never paid her directly, George himself making up the difference in cash. For that matter when it came to paying, neither did the police commissioner nor any of the city aldermen who in silent collusion kept the house protected from the law and managed to find a myriad of excuses for dropping by at all hours to inspect the premises, check for illegal gambling and give

66

occasional lip service to the Women's Purity Committees, a luncheon group of Manhattan's finest society matrons dedicated to cleaning the decadence from the Streets of New York…and more lunches.

George O'Keefe was careful not to rock the boat down at City Hall, as it was their willful compliance that fed his golden goose. He donated heavily to the police, fire department, and the Tammany Hall Democratic Club. New York City was a town renowned for selling both commerce and vice in huge quantities while virtue lay in scant supply. Even during the war of succession from England, the city had shared little of the revolutionary fervor of Boston and Philadelphia (both cities later turning to religious and abolitionist zeal) and a majority of the city's population had remained blatantly pro-British and willingly entertained General Howe and his red-coated staff of officers in their homes. And more lately, the whole country was still reeling from Manhattan's disgraceful reaction to Abe Lincoln's call to arms in 1863: a full fledged draft riot and the lynching of Negroes which finally left twelve hundred dead and only abated after long suffering Abe pulled thirteen regiments of Federal Troops off the front lines to restore order in this, the most northern of the cities of the Union. Ever since George Washington snidely referred to it as 'The Empire City, New York's reputation as a rapacious megalopolis seemed only to grow worse as its fortunes grew greater.

What the mayor's office did in the sense of civic propriety and to satisfy the touchy first families - the Vanderbilt's and Astor's - was a city wide sweep on illegal gambling from time to time accompanied by a police raid of the house in full public view after, of course, forewarning George O'Keefe so that he might send his flock of girls over to Hoboken on the Jersey side of the Hudson River to avoid the invasion of the constabulary. With a meager catch of a few inebriated dockworkers rounded up while playing cards, a large procession of police carriages would make much ado about hauling the poor souls into prison for the night. At least this way, the local society matrons might fool themselves into believing that it was nothing more than an itch for card playing that was keeping their wandering husbands out late once, twice or, in the case of the mayor, three times a week.

When Petit Jean arrived at the Hudson Ferry pier on the Jersey side of the river with his small bag of possessions - some odd clothes, a game of jacks, a few family mementos and his father's silver Derringer - he apprehensively surveyed the wide water full of racing currents unable to imagine how this flat bottomed ferry would ever make it safely across. Even from the far side of the river the boy sensed he could actually smell and feel the swarming city arising on the far shore - the smoke from the factories and the teams of heavy horses delivering milk and coal. His excitement so overcame his anxiety that he nearly would have swum the rest of the way just to get sooner into the midst of all that tumultuous activity. It had taken him long enough to get to New Jersey - close to a month's time coming from Vendee, crossing Kansas and Missouri sitting in the back of a supply wagon and then from St. Louis and on to Pittsburgh, huddling in the third class compartment of trains and coaches until he reached this very spot with the slums of New York Island popping up in front of him like a crop of smoky upturned cigars.

His ma had been crying and already half drunk the day he left Vendee, but she stood there unsteadily holding onto Father Bachet and promised her son two things: first, that she would send for him in a year or two at most, and two, that she would stop drinking; neither of which promises she kept. Antoinette was silently holding a grimy doll in her hand, its head resting in the muddy road while the supply wagon waited for him to climb aboard. Petit Jean bent down to kiss his little sister and whispered his own promise into the ear: that he would someday return to avenge their daddy's death. He sat in the back of that wagon and watched Vendee fade from view, never shedding a single tear nor waving back to his family.

Now as the New York ferry rocked and rolled its way across the wide Hudson the masts of all the freighters and clipper ships in the harbor came clearly into view. Once disembarked, Petit Jean immediately ran up to the first trustworthy looking man he could find: a tall, gray bearded, retired skipper called Captain Al, who sat on a mooring stump and chewed on a corncob pipe, still wearing his brass buttoned captain's uniform.

"Excuse me sir? Can you help me sir?" asked Petit Jean timidly.

"What be it boy? Speak up, but I've got no ship to bring a cabin boy aboard," the captain replied.

"No sir. I'm just coming off a boat myself I reckon, and I'm looking for my Uncle and I don't know where to start looking," Petit Jean took the rumpled piece of paper that Father Bachet had written out for him out of the homespun overcoat he was already outgrowing.

"George O'Keefe!" Said captain Al. "My, but you look a wee bit young for that kind of goings on to me."

"Sir?"

"Ah, come along boy. I'll show you where you might find him."

Captain Al and Petit Jean walked up Canal Street until they were along side the impressive red brick building with the wide veranda and brightly painted sign. Red lanterns - lit even in daytime - decorated every upstairs window that faced out onto 23rd Street.

"They use to call this district *Satan's Circus* when I first came ashore here from New Province, Rhode Island a lifetime ago. I guess you could say that since then it has managed to gentrify itself somewhat, merely to be called the bloody *Tenderloin*. Anything you may want in this town - that is anything outside of religion - you'll be finding in the Tenderloin. There you go boy - this be the infamous house of your Uncle George O'Keefe's that I'm sorry to say I know the way to so very well."

"But why all the red lanterns sir?" Asked Petit Jean.

"Oh its come to be a symbol of...welcome, I reckon is the best way I can put it, boy. Some say the railroad men started leaving them there back when the girls would set up in tents behind the Illinois Central Line and by the time those boys left they was too damn relaxed - or maybe drunk - and just forgot to take 'em on their way out, but others say it was General

70

Hooker's boys." The old captain laughed. "Let's go inside boy. Maybe my old blood will get stirring again, if only from imagining what others can do and I cannot anymore. Ah, it's the irony of life that when a man reaches an age where nearly every women who crosses his sight is desirable he has not the power inside him to please her."

Not really understanding what the old sea captain was talking about, Petit Jean followed him as they walked up the stairs to the porch and swung the swiveled brass mermaid who's naked breasts' patina shone smooth from hundreds of men's sweating, anticipating hands. Young Qwing So, who stood a head shorter than Petit Jean and was dressed in a schoolgirl's blue frock with her long black braid hanging halfway down her back, opened the door, curtsying politely and showing them to one of the set tables off the bar.

"We're here to see George O'Keefe, missy," said the captain. "The proprietor of this...restaurant," he giggled.

The girl mumbled something in Cantonese and looked at Petit Jean quizzically for a moment as if to ask what might he be doing in here, looking as out of place as her, before scurrying off. The captain and the boy sat down at one of the front tables. "So where do you come from boy? Somewhere up in Acadia I would suspect by your accent. Off the coast of Newfoundland?"

"No, sir. I come by Vendee in Old Oklahoma just across from the Cherokee Nation but my ma's people came from up that way, Acadia up north and than down through Vermont to Long Island. But it was my pa who brought her out west."

"And your Pa? He'd be Arcadian too I reckon?" asked the captain.

"Well...I think he came over from Ireland with his brother George, my uncle."

"His brother George? Well I'll be...so George O'Keefe *is* really your uncle after all."

"I guess that'd be right sir."

"And where's your Pa now?" Asked the Captain. "Will he be coming along for a visit himself shortly I suppose?"

"No, sir...my pa won't be coming. He's..."

Petit Jean's painful explanation was interrupted by the commotion of one huge man bounding down the short flight of stairs next to the bar. George O'Keefe seemed to take up twice as much space as God had generously afforded him to begin with and, on first sight, Petit Jean thought him a spitting image of the pictures of Santa Claus his ma had shown him every Christmas, with his red cheeks, white beard and long white hair. George O'Keefe was flamboyantly dressed in a black velvet suit, bright red vest and black riding jodhpurs, although it had been years since any unlucky horse had suffered under his weight. Even so, he carried a stiff riding crop in his right hand. Not that he hit anybody with it - at least not too often - but it had become his symbolic truncheon of arms and he was apt to punctuate any story he might recount with a series of sharp curts onto the leather uppers of his boots.

When he reached the landing of the stairs, the huge man stood gazing over the empty barroom with an immediate, threatening air of authority: Hank the barman started drying glasses rapidly and old Captain Al managed to choke on his pipe as George put him under his stern gaze before being able to spurt out some utterance, some explanation of why he was taking up space in George's precious establishment that afternoon.

"Excuse me for barging in on you like this, George," said Captain Al timidly. "Such a fine afternoon and all…but this young lad came upon me down at the docks and asked me the way to your place so I figured I'd take him myself."

"Have you lost your mind now completely, you sea-logged old goat? This is no place for a lost child," George O'Keefe snarled. "Take him down to the foundling house, they can better deal with a waif like him then I can here for God's sake."

"Yes, George, of course George…" Captain Al gulped hard before he continued. "But the boy here, he be saying that you are his very own uncle, his own flesh and blood I tell you, so I thought it my duty to at least show him the way to you and make sure that he came to no harm before he was under your charge. You wouldn't mind offering me a round of Ale for my troubles would you George?"

Now, George O'Keefe was a man held in rare esteem by all the rough and tumble men who frequented the New York harbor; respected even by seamen who had sailed through treacherous typhoons, witnessed waterspouts as high as a ship's mast and been boarded by murdering pirates off the Barbary coast. Because even the most fearless among brave

73

men such as these could not imagine anything as daunting, as downright terrifying, as managing a half-dressed crew of jabbering whores while making a handsome profit to boot. Simply how a man kept his own sanity under such conditions was a mystery to them all. Admired and feared, George O'Keefe remained an enigma to the men folk of Manhattan and few chose to test his patience, as he did not suffer fools easily. But when this formidable presence of a man saw his own dead brother's boy before him, trembling at the mere sight of him, his fearsome hazel eyes watered over and he cried out:

"Oh my God, if it isn't the spitting image of Johnny O'Keefe standing before me. Its as if my own dead brother has come back, Jesus and all the saints be praised. Come here boy and let me take a look at you for Christ's sakes. You got nothing to fear from me."

Petit Jean stood up from his chair and slowly approached the giant man standing at the foot of the stairs. When he got within arms length, George O'Keefe reached out and picked the boy up right off his feet and embraced him so hard the boy thought his lungs would collapse, the tears now freely rolling down his uncle's cheeks. And at the same time Petit Jean was hoping his uncle would never let him go.

George O'Keefe could be a violent man, as dangerous when provoked as any rogue in New York City and he had thrown more than a few drunks over the balcony of his bordello to crash onto the tables below if they had the gall to manhandle any of his girls and risk damaging what he considered to be his own personal property. But when he lifted

74

the boy off his feet, nearly hugging all the breath out of him before setting Petit Jean back on his feet again, his heartstrings had been pulled so strongly that he was moved to tears.

"Oh Johnny," he wailed. "My poor dead brother who I'll never set eyes on again until we meet again in Paradise. I can feel your presence here with me now, and you've brought your only son to me like a miraculous resurrection. Its almost too much for a grown man to bare."

"What do you suppose on doing with the lad?" Asked Captain Al sipping down his glass of ale. "Send him down to the orphanage, I suppose?"

While still spellbound by the boy, George O'Keefe took a step forward and with a swing of his brawny leg kicked the chair right out from under Captain Al who went flying onto his rump and came up spitting and choking, his glass full of ale halfway down his throat.

"With God as my witness this boy will never see the inside of one of those foul establishments as long as I'm alive. I've still got the scars on my own back from the whips of the priests who ran the wretched place in Boston where his father Johnny and I spend the most miserable years of our miserable young lives."

"I'm sure sorry to offend you, George." Captain Al slowly and painfully got onto his feet. "No disrespect meant...I mean I was just wondering what with all your...girls and all...you know. What would the boy be doing here?"

"I dare say that what I've got here is no different than that what fills

75

up half the Academy of Music balcony each and every Opera season," said George. "Only difference being that my girls don't wear wedding rings." He belched out a huge laugh. "Now tell me boy, what do you call yourself now?"

"My ma calls me Petit Jean."

"Well, Petit Jean it is then, and a grand welcome to O'Keefe's Emporium. Consider yourself to have the run of the place, son. And if any man tries to give you the business they'll be hearing from me in no time flat. You get the word around Captain Al, eh? Any man who harms this boy will just as well be harming me and he will pay a fearsome price."

"Sure enough, George. That I will do."

Then George O'Keefe hauled the boy up the stairs for grand introductions to all his whores who made a rousing fuss over Petit Jean, mothering him like some poor lost orphan sent by the lord himself for them to protect from the horrors of the world. These women who had all been robbed of their own childhood in some poor fashion - nearly all raped or abandoned – and left with few other means of survival besides a kind of benevolent sexual slavery, they welcomed the boy into their midst with warmth and sincerity, a refreshing distraction from the monotony of un-bathed sailors and the daily angst of what might happen to them once their looks started to fade and their charm wore thin.

Within days Petit Jean had the run of the place and was bringing clean towels and washbowls of warm water to the girls in their rooms, refilling the piano player's whisky glass and running to fetch cigars and newspapers for clients waiting in the dining room down below. He kept his tips in a cigar box under the bed in his own little room up in the attic that Uncle George had set up for him. Over his bed hung a faded photograph of his pa and ma on their wedding day, his father smiling, has mother looking scared. And under his pillow was his father's Derringer.

It didn't take long for Petit Jean to begin to suspect that was something going on at Uncle George's *restaurant* that Father Bachet would surely not approve of and that it was happening somewhere up in all those bedrooms that lined the halls of the two floors above the bar. But still, he couldn't quite grasp what exactly it was, what force, that could motivate all those men to find their way to the house at all hours no matter how bad the weather might be and with nothing decent even to eat in there. Of course, he enjoyed talking with the girls himself but it wouldn't keep him from hanging out on the docks and watching the tall ships enter the harbor.

Of all the girls, Petit Jean's favorite was Barbara Banner. He had never in his life seen a woman with skin so clean looking, so creamy that he imagined she must have gotten it that way just from washing it over and over with the precious bars of honey soap she kept in her toilette. Calling her Missy Banner he would bring her a glass of lemonade as she sat in front of her vanity mirror giving her long chestnut hair a hundred strokes with her monogrammed hairbrush. She looked so delicate and fragile, as breakable as fine porcelain except when she summoned up the roaring laugh which lay deep inside her prim facade when something struck her deliriously funny and then her mouth could open so wide that you could notice her horsy overbite. But times of such hilarity were rare with Missy Banner and normally she stayed true to her melancholy nature.

Still, Barbara Banner was the queen bee of George O'Keefe's house and she knew it well enough. Although she put on airs of being civil to the other girls, she could easily fly into a rage if she found any of her tortoise shell hairpins missing or if another girl had the nerve to borrow a pair of her silk hose without asking. Such luxuries were not new to Missy Banner; she was an exile from the rich Georgia coast and her family had owned and worked a large plantation outside Savannah for generations until it was burned to the ground during General Sherman's terror march to the sea, only two lonely chimney stacks left standing. Because her father was a Colonel fighting with the Confederate army under General Robert E. Lee Army of Northern Virginia, the advance troops of Sherman's cavalry thought it their duty to confiscate everything they might find on any confirmed rebel's property, and that included young Barbara herself, all of sixteen years old. Caught carrying two buckets of well water one moonless night, she was dragged backed to the river's edge where no less than fifteen drunken soldiers gang raped her before she managed to crawl away and hide in the brush. She was found collapsed and incoherent on the doorstep of a rebel sympathizer when the sun came up the following morning. Her mother stitched up the poor girl's damaged sex and Barbara lay in bed for a month where her violet bruises and black eyes could heal out of proper Savannah society's view. Barbara promised herself that from that day onward, any other man who took her again would surely pay a price - money or his life; she swore would die before she became any man's free sport again.

When Colonel Banner did not return after the war, Barbara was sent north by her mother to search for him among the Confederate prisoners. She never did find out the fate of her father whose body was decomposing in Appomattox field, but she did catch the eye of a New York news reporter from The Herald who offered her room and board in his hotel room in over-crowded Washington DC and promised to bring her up north to New York with him if she would let him have his way with her which she did - for a price. She still carried the original gold coin that Herald reporter gave here as a talisman of luck.

It was Qwing So's job to haul all the washing down to a German lady's laundry twice a week while the girls sat around and waited often in nothing more then sheets and towels until their lingerie was brought back clean and white later that afternoon. The little Chinese girl who rarely spoke loud enough to be noticed could actually speak English far better than her three sisters as well as rapid-fire Cantonese but she quickly became Petit Jean's playmate and confidant, and the two ran freely around the neighborhood together, playing hide and seek, hoops, and cowboys and Indians, just like the boy had played with his sister Antoinette back in Vendee. The whores enjoyed playing with Qwing So as well and sometimes they would braid her hair and dress her up with makeup, splashing her with perfume as she stopped from room to room to pick up soiled sheets and night clothes. Old Nell commented on the girl's tiny feet each time she saw them and for a time started binding her own in huge wads of linen in the ancient Chinese fashion, hoping that they might shrink from her own gargantuan size twelve.

Chapter 7

Where better to learn the practical matters of sex than in a whorehouse where the daily ins and outs of the trade are no less hydraulic or mundane then a plumber's skill? Or would that be like trying to educate your palate for the subtleties of various *cuisine de poisson* while pulling fish guts out on a trawler in the North Atlantic? But it was there, in the midst of a working Bordello, where fourteen-year old Petit Jean was to be drawn into the four dark corners of the world of Eros and see sights that would both delight and haunt him the rest of his life. And it was old Captain Al himself who finally breached the subject and told Petit Jean the facts of life, as best as he could remember them himself, early one evening sitting in the bar alone while Petit Jean scrubbed the floor around him.

Captain Al was listening to the moans of yearning drifting down the stairway when he caught sight of Petit Jean's concerned expression as he too gazed toward the rooms beyond the balcony and the thought gripped him that the boy might know nothing of what was happening around him.

"Tell me boy, do ye have any idea what's going on in more than a few of the rooms on the floors above us?"

"I suppose Miss Banner is having a gentleman caller for a game of cards?" He asked.

"I don't think its cards they be playing upstairs. They are playing with nature's most basic urge. Boy, did I ever tell you about my first voyage to the South Pacific? To the paradise islands of Tahiti where the women run naked and the men be always smiling? My but those pretty coffee colored lasses knew how to welcome a lonesome sailor so far from home. I swear to you I never saw so many naked bodies of the female species in my life, never imagined that a woman's breasts could be formed in so many shapes and sizes. It was an education that I'll remember till my last dying day."

"Are you saying that you married one of these gals from down Tahiti way Captain Al?"

"I tell you boy, I should have jumped ship then and there and lived out my days under palm trees."

But it was on the return trip that Captain Al had finally lost his own virginity in a whore house in Lisbon where he was so drunk on Port that he little remembered what happened, and a western woman, even a whore, was not as inclined to put her private parts on display as freely as the guilt-free native girls of Tahiti. Petit Jean followed the old man's story as best he could, wondering all the time what the point of it all was. The captain could ramble on and on and often would pigeonhole the boy for hours with endless tales from his sailing days. The boy did know something about pigs and horses and cows jumping on top of each other, and chickens sitting on their eggs, but what any of that had to do with what was going on in those ladies' rooms upstairs he just couldn't figure out for the life of him.

"You see son," said Captain Al. "It's just a hankering a man gets sometimes. And he never knows when it might be coming. Someday you might wake up with that hankering and it stays with you all day itching like a bad mosquito bite, 'cept its a good kinda itch. Other times you might get it in the strangest damn places. Once, it even happened to me in church."

"In church?" said Petit Jean. "I never got bit by no mosquito in church - a bee once stung my little sister Antoinette, but..."

"No boy! You're missing the whole point. It's the hankering that's important. It doesn't matter where you might catch it."

"What do you mean?" Said Petit Jean. "A hankering for what?"

"Well, for a woman, of course lad. Its like an itch a man gets and only the touch of the female of the species can scratch it. Now I'm sorry to say, me and you, we're neither one of us capable of itching for a woman - you ain't even started yet and my own scratching days are over. But you, you'll see boy, you'll be peeking in those keyholes before long."

"And what be through these keyholes worth peeking at?" Asked Petit Jean.

From upstairs wafted down the not so small sounds of grunts and groans of male satisfaction. At first, Petit Jean, thought that the old man was just kidding him, making up another one of his fantastical stories like those of the hair covered monkey men of Madagascar. He was anxious to finish mopping down the floor so he might start up a game of hoops with Qwing So out on 23rd Street.

Captain Al took a furtive look around the bar: the piano player was sleeping on the ivory keys and Hank the bartender was engrossed in some dime novel as he absentmindedly shined the same wine glass over and over. The captain gave Petit Jean a conspiratorial wink. "Follow me boy," and he headed up the stairs as silently as his rickety old legs could carry him. At the end of the red-carpeted hall, faintly lit by gas burning brass lamps, the captain put his ear to the door and turned around and smiled at the boy, "I think we picked a winner," he whispered. "It's old Nell - they call her the toothless wonder." Captain Al bent down and put his eye to the keyhole for a minute before dropping to his knees and taking off his pilot's cap and rubbing his handkerchief across his sweaty brow. "Oh lord, can't you just give me enough strength for one night more..."

Petit Jean crawled in front of the Captain Al and put his own eye right on the keyhole. The heavy curtains were drawn over the windows but the room was still illuminated by the glowing candelabra next to the bed. It looked like the two people on the bed were playing some sort of a game, something like bobbing for apples, except soon the boy saw that Nell was on her knees with her top naked and her ample breasts shaking with a gravity all their own. One of his Uncle's customers, he couldn't tell whom, was lying on his back with his hands behind his head, moaning low. But Petit Jean could see no bucket of apples on the bed and when Nell backed away from the naked man reclining on her bed to catch her breath, what she held in her hand was the likes of what Petit Jean had never seen before, something like his own pecker, but standing up straight as a one-eyed prairie dog just out of its hole. And when Nell bent back over the man's hips and put his whole pecker right back into her mouth the boy thought he must be watching some sort of sorcery.

"Dear God!" said Petit Jean. "She must be some kind of witch! She'll choke to death on that thing."

"Don't you worry about ol' Nell," said the captain. "She's got less teeth than me and I don't think she'll be choking to death tonight."

With a great deal of his Uncle George's help Petit Jean wrote regular letters back to his mother in Vendee; letters that described his life on Manhattan Island in a sanitized version far from reality: his Uncle George a man of character and pure charity, a stalwart of the best society of New York who ran a clean and honest residence for the homeless young girls he found on the cruel streets of New York.

Petit Jean went so far as to describe a regular morning mass, attended by George and his girls as well as by Petit Jean, Qwing So and Captain Al, thinking this would please his mother and particularly Father Bachet. The truth was that Uncle George had been refused communion for years by the local priest until he first submitted to a lengthy confession, but, as George so bluntly put it, he'd be damned before he shared his "business secrets" with anyone - not even a priest. In frustration, the priest himself began a habit of confessing Uncle George's sins himself to anybody who'd listen while sanctimoniously proclaiming that he would rather put the symbolic flesh and blood of the savior right into the mouth of the devil himself than in the sinful gorge of kneeling George O'Keefe. Of course, this didn't keep George and his girls from showing up for Midnight Mass

85

each Christmas Eve, decked out in their finest silks and velvets, strolling down the church aisle like a flock of ducklings, heads bowed meekly behind the imposing figure of George O'Keefe to the wide eyed stares of the kneeling parishioners. In the spirit of the season, the priest chose to ignore the presence of Uncle George's and his entourage for this one joyous day, and the rather large donation of gold coins that George set in the basket passed his way during the singing of Noel carols, did seem to earn him at least one day of absolution per year.

But conversely, when it came to that part of his life he had left out west, the letters that Petit Jean received from his mother were, he only could hope, far worse in tone than the real situation back in Vendee. His family's farm had indeed been sold to an anonymous buyer and now his ma was living in the church itself with Antoinette and generally serving Father Bachet's needs, cleaning the ministry which now also served the few Mexican families come north from Texas as well as some recently converted Kiowa Indians. In nearly every letter he received from his mother would be an attached note from Father Bachet carefully listing the expenses of keeping Antoinette and Petit Jean's ma and asking if Uncle George might find it in his heart to send back a slight donation to help offset the costs of the church's charity. Uncle George would grunt to himself while sitting at his roll top desk and more often than not send back a few gold eagles by return mail.

The boy was starting to ask Uncle George more and more about his father, about the grandparents who he never knew and about the War

Between the States in which both his uncle and father fought. Come Sunday afternoon, George would take the boy for a walk by the docks with the sharp smell of the harbor and the calling of the gulls overhead and try to explain to Petit Jean just who his kin were and where he had come from.

"Your pa's and my parents fled the terrible Irish famine in 1840 like nearly one third of their starving countryman had done when the damned British refused to give their grain reserves to the starving people. Some found their way across the Irish Sea to nearby Liverpool to work in the great shipyards there; and some others were more anxious to get as far away from the damn Brits as possible and take the long voyage down to Australia. But like me own parents the vast majority headed straight across the Atlantic Ocean for America, where a man could be free to starve on his own not needing the bloody British to help him along to his grave. They set their sights on Boston, to be exact boy."

The parents of John and George, themselves barely adults, had starved themselves so dearly to be able to afford the fare of the voyage for all four of them, that they really were in no shape at all for such journey and when a wave of cholera broke out on the ship they were among the first to fall victim. They two arrived in Boston harbor more dead than alive but miraculously their two boys, George and Johnny, had escaped the scourge and were quickly separated from their ailing parents. Some days later, the boys were told that both their parents had died in quarantine, never really setting foot in the free new world.

"At least they died with the comfort of knowing that their young sons would grow up to be fine Americans," added the U.S. immigration officer somewhat ingenuously.

However, the price of the two boys' freedom did not come cheap. They were auctioned off to a workhouse run under the auspices of a Catholic Church orphanage that was really just another profit making factory for one of the old Brahmin families who ran Boston. When George reached the age of sixteen, he was sent to work in the mills with the admonition that the devil would cut off the hands of any boy whose thoughts strayed from the work of the day and with the dangerous whirring machines just inches away from fingers and hands, it was not uncommon for a blood curdling scream to cut through the tediousness of the ten hour days. In two years, young Johnny reached his own working age and joined George at the orphanage attached to the mill, where whippings by the priests were a regular occurrence.

"Me, being the oldest, I tried to protect me little brother Johnny from the priests' ferocious straps but even back then his temper was his worst enemy. So we got by as best we could but then, soon after Abe Lincoln's inauguration, the rebel's canons shelled the federal Fort Sumter in Charleston harbor. Boston broke out in pure celebration as if God himself had proclaimed the rebel's succession as a joyous event rather than the start of a carnage the world had not seen before."

Boston took pride in starting the war, as many of the great abolitionist of the day came from the city and a large share of Bostonians felt it their moral right to lead the country - and particularly the king cotton southern states - out of sinful slavery. To the abolitionists of the day, the westerner Abe Lincoln was a too recent and untrustworthy devotee to their cause: a compromising politician who would easily sell out the radical Republicans who had brought him to power if it meant he might enjoy the comforts of the White House for another four years.

"Johnny and I up and enlisted in the 69th Massachusetts division and we immediately caught hell at the second battle of Antietem and again at Chancellorsville. Then in the frenzy of the battle we were cut off from our regiment and captured by the retreating rebels and eventually they sent the two of us down to the hellhole of Andersonville prison camp in Georgia.

"If there is a hell it couldn't be worse than that god forsaken place," said Uncle George. "We were treated lower than the rats - at least they ate better - and there was a meanness to the guards that held no reason or rhyme. They hated us for being Irish and Yankees to boot, even though the both of us had only been in the damn country for less than ten years. I remember one son of a bitch rebel officer, some dandy from New Orleans named Durand, who had it in for all us Yankees. He'd take away a man's boots on the first day of winter just to see the frost bite set in and took a special pleasure into spitting down the prisoners drinking well each time he passed it."

"Durand?" Petit Jean gulped hard. "Not Judge Abel Durand?"

"Well son, back in Andersonville he was more than a mere judge – Christ, he was nearly the judge, jury and executioner. Sent more than a few poor Yankee souls to meet their maker I might add. If there's a God in heaven than that man is rotting in hell as we speak."

"Well, if Vendee be hell, I guess you be right about that," said Petit Jean.

"What's that boy?"

Petit Jean couldn't bring himself to tell his father's brother about Durand yet, nor of his own sacred promise to avenge his pa's death. And he feared that by telling anybody of the pledge he had solemnly made to himself would somehow take all the strength and magic out of it.

"Nothing Uncle...tell me about my ma. Were you there when they met?"

"Well, us soldiers we were on our way back up north to be discharged and a bunch of us were bivouacked out on Long Island waiting for the ferry to come take us back to Massachusetts. That was when Johnny met your mother. She was working at her father's Inn in the harbor where we would come to drink and well, you know how it is, he and your ma were just made for each other. She was a pretty French milkmaid with flaming red hair and this Frenchy accent that just drove him wild. She was really something - I'll never forget she use to carry a poem in her pocket - said it was written for her by none other than Walt Whitman and she wouldn't show it to anyone. He tended the union wounded and dying during the war, you know. Did you ever hear of the man, son?"

"Its the only name from back east asides from you and my grandpa that I'm acquainted with. But what was my ma like back then?"

"She was sure a beauty, your mother, and there was no holding your pa back. The lieutenant in charge of the brigade being a kindhearted sort discharged him right then and there and already he was talking of going out west – in fact he started planning it while we were still in Andersonville. I imagine those dreams probably helped keep him alive."

"And what did you do Uncle? Why didn't you go west?"

"Me? You know son, I had had enough adventure for one lifetime during the god-awful war without heading out into that Indian infested god forsaken territory. I was just looking to settle down someplace comfortable and make some money so I'd be something more than just another down and out *mick*. In Boston, they was hating us Irish too much for me to get anywhere but back into the damn factory I had just come out of, but down here in New York I heard there were already a few boys from County Cork who had gotten themselves pretty thick into the local politics of the city, so I headed down here myself and hooked up with them as best I could. And when the chance came for me to buy into this, this…little bar, by the docks I jumped at it. With the help of a few silent partners, of course."

"But didn't you miss seeing Pa."

"Well, son there comes a time when brothers have a parting of the ways and must say goodbye and each make their own way in the world if they're ever to know what kind of men they really are. Your father was a fair man but too easy to set his jaw in an argument, like a dog that gets a bone between its teeth and can't let it go. I suppose that's what happened out west, except he crossed the wrong man. If only I'd a been there to keep him out of trouble."

"Pa was murdered," blurted out Petit Jean. "They shot him when he weren't looking."

"But I thought it was a fair fight," said Uncle George. "Your ma wrote and said he challenged one of the local gunmen to a duel."

"Well, I ain't never seen no duel," said Petit Jean. "So I don't reckon I know what one looks like, but I was right there in that saloon with him and he had no chance at all. Pa never fired a shot."

"Never fired a shot! What in God's name happened then?"

"Pa never took Judge Durand seriously, he was walking away from the table when a shot from Durand went whizzing past his head. But it was another man who kilt him. On Durand's order's I suppose." Petit Jean chomped his teeth tight together; it was the only way to keep from crying. "That bastard Judge Durand missed him by a mile and than lied at the hearing. It was his hired man Carpis who done it."

"Durand?" Said Uncle George stunned. "It couldn't be the same...why I thought they hung that man in Washington after the war, I'm sure. What did he look like, this Judge Durand?"

"I'd say not too much older than you. With a bum leg he bragged was some kind of battle wound."

"By hell he got that limp in the war! He was born that way. We figured that's what made him so god damn mean. So poor Johnny met up

92

with that son of a bitch Durand again. If only..." George spit into the Hudson River. "So help me god there will be a day of reckoning with that miserable bastard from New Orleans!"

Now, Petit Jean was sorry he had told him uncle what happened, he felt as if he had lost some part of himself, given something away. At least he had kept his own promise of revenge a secret. He was glad of that.

Chapter 8

Walt Whitman sat at his desk in his small frame house in Camden, New Jersey and grasped in his hands a photograph of himself taken nearly twenty years earlier, posed in a white open necked shirt and with a jaunty and adventurous air about him. His hands trembled and he moaned for his lost youth, for his stamina and his innocence. He was fifty-three years old and various maladies of the last ten years had left him palsied and weak. He was expecting a visitor that day, one Edward Carpenter, an English admirer and poetic scholar who adored the poet and sang his praises continually both to his face and to anyone else who would listen. But even with his effervescent fountain of compliments and genteel manners, Whitman still found him somewhat of a bore and he longed for the rough workingmen he had befriended in Brooklyn and on the New York docks. Walt Whitman was constantly besieged by visitors now, be it eager young disciples from Harvard or distinguished scholars from Europe - all anxious to press the hand of the renowned American poet of the people, the bard of democracy. Whitman himself had always preferred the casual company of working class companions who neither read his poetry nor anyone else's, street car drivers and the like, over that of constipated academics and moralist crusaders. But his celebrity had come so late in his life after all those years of tirelessly slogging his books door to door and often being the sole if tireless promoter of his own works. In fact, on more than one occasion, it was he himself who sold his works door to door and then would write an accompanying, glowing review in the Brooklyn newspapers he worked for at the time. So now, at this advanced stage in life, he patiently suffered nearly any admirer who chose to be in his presence, content to be finally taken seriously by any public other than he himself.

Whitman was six feet in height, weighed nearly two hundred pounds, and even with his various maladies still held himself very straight with an erect posture. His long, very fine snowy white hair made him appear older than he was and he walked feebly owing to an earlier paralysis - but still his high arched eyebrows gave him an air of childlike wonder and contemplation. At other times his heavily lidded eyes, laying far back in his head, gave him that *wild hawk* look the English thought common to self made Americans such as him and Abraham Lincoln.

In 1884 he had moved to this address on Mickle Street - his own house at last after years of living with his brother, also in Camden. There was a smelly Guano factory across the river, for which he was perversely grateful as it kept the more gentile visitors from prolonging their visits to an intolerable length. Waiting until the stench was particularly strong he would than extend a feeble dinner invitation, rarely worried that it might be accepted. But after the stench of the dead and dying in the Civil War hospitals in which he had worked as a male nurse, a gust of guano did not faze him in the least.

Portraits of Whitman's mother and father hung over his bed as he sat in a huge cane chair between two windows, his back warming to a small coal burning stove in his bedroom on the second floor. It was some minutes before he finally became aware of the gentle knocking on his front door and he painfully straightened and descended the stairs to answer. When he pulled the door open and saw the boy standing there alone, he stood staring and blinking, uncomprehending for this was not the overly ingratiating presence of Edward Carpenter he had been expecting. The boy was handsome with an attractive nervous air about him, around sixteen years old he imagined. "Am I lucky today?" He thought trying to control his excitement.

As for Petit Jean, when he had begun his search for Walt Whitman he was surprised at the reverence with which so many spoke the name, even if to his own mother the poet was something of a saint and even if it was true that in his declining years the old sage had taken on near divine status. Petit Jean looked up anxiously at the old man who slowly swung open the door and lasciviously stared back at him. This didn't look like any great personage to him, like a famous poet should look. Actually the old gent in front of him sort of resembled old Captain Al, but then again the only great personage he had ever met, he imagined, was his Uncle George and he supposed this must be the caretaker of the house.

"This be Mickle Street, Camden, New Jersey?" Asked Petit Jean, standing in the doorway, holding the scrap of paper in front of him where he had scribbled the address.

"Yes son, there is no other Mickel Street in Camden but this one and no other Camden in New Jersey but this one and no other New Jersey that I know of in this universe but this one as well."

"And is there a great poet living here by the name of Whitman - Walt being his given name?" asked Petit Jean.

"There is a Whitman living here son and one who would also dare so presumes to call himself a poet. And there are no other poets in Camden or at least living on Mickel Street that I am aware of, so I imagine you have found your man. Although this universe with all its mystery might have put me living next to the great bard William Shakespeare himself and I suppose I wouldn't be privy to it."

"Shakespeare?" Asked Petit Jean. "Is he a friend of this here Whitman fellow?"

"I suppose we'll have to leave that decision to the ages," said Whitman. "Why don't you come in my boy? My bones are weary and there's a chill in the air."

"Don't mind if I do, sir," said Petit Jean. "As long as you promise me you can roust this Whitman fellow from wherever he may be hiding."

Walt Whitman laughed and his eyes sparkled above his gray beard. "You need look no further boy for I am the very same Walt Whitman you have mentioned. Him and I are the same, I'm sorry to say."

Petit Jean entered the small house still doubting that this wiry old gent could be the great man himself. Whitman showed him into the parlor room and when he perused a copy of *Leaves Of Grass* lying open to its half title page, with the daguerreotype of Whitman in his younger days staring

97

back at him, he knew if only from the look in the eyes that this old gent showing him to his chair was one and the same. Walt Whitman himself.

All around the room were books, manuscripts, letters, paper, magazines, parcels tied up with bits of string, photographs and literary material; some piled nearly a yard high on a little table stood in danger of toppling any minute into the two or three overflowing wastebaskets. Petit Jean waded through this sea of disorder to find a chair. But Whitman directed him to sit on the day bed by the window next to him.

"How can I help you son? Do I know you from somewhere?"

"In fact we never met, sir, but I think you knew my ma, some years ago before I was born. That's why I come to see you, to bring her hellos I guess, and to ask you to write something to her so I might send it in a letter. You see, my pa died a while back so now she's got no husband and seems to be kind of lost without him. And you mean a lot to her, it seems. Maybe you're the only thing keeps her hanging on to this life."

"And who be your ma, boy? She comes from Camden town or from over the river in Philadelphia?"

"No sir, my ma come from Huntington Harbor out on Long Island and she says that you was hanging about her pa's tavern from time to time when she was growing up there - said she use to serve you her own pa's cooking herself - said she remembers you liking his cooking well enough though I don't suppose she could be to sure of that, never having lived inside your gullet."

"You're a strange boy to be thinking thoughts like that, reminds me of myself when I was your age. Always searching for the common human thread as it were. Still not sure if I ever found it..."

The old poet closed his eyes imagining the Long Island of his own youth: the Hempstead plains and the endless dune caped beaches of the outer islets of the south shore.

"Paumanok," he said quietly and then he begin reciting: "Sea-Beauty! Stretch'd and basking! Isle of the salty shore and breeze and brine!"

"What that mean sir? Paumanok? Sounds like an injun word to me."

"That it is son, from the old Delawares themselves who were masters of the land before the Dutch and English set foot on terra firma. Means laid against the sea. Beautiful word isn't it?"

"Can't say that the injuns I knew had much to say about anything - not the ones I met back in Oklahoma Territory anyhow. Kind of kept to themselves, if you ask me."

"Ah yes! They are a closed-mouthed lot to be sure - maybe to their better. But did you know there was once a famous Indian preacher - Samson Occum - preaching the word of the white man's God himself out on Long Island? Quite celebrated in his time - they say he even visited London, England and became quite a personage in his own right - preached in Whitefield's church in genuine Indian dialect, no less."

"Excuse me, but did you know her, sir? Did you know my ma?"

"Well, back in those days, I use to take many a jaunt for days on end back to Paumanok - to Long Island. Had a ready stock of walking energy back then and would follow it wherever it took me - out to Greenport or

Montauk even, the twin ends of the fishtailed island, tagging along on fishing ships or testing out the early line of the Long Island Railroad. Rails laid pure and straight out through the Hempstead Plains - all that open land within thirty miles from the city - and on through the brush of Hicksville and the old Quakers of Jericho - and still that damn train never did run on time. But the colors of the island in God's chemistry of autumn is exceedingly beautiful, son. Deep and pale red, the green most often pines, the bright yellow of the hickory. Always thought of using it for carpet designs. Could have made a bundle don't you think?"

"Don't know much about carpets or bundles sir"

"Did you ever fish for the black-fish boy? Biting famously every fall out of Greenport? One time we jumped onto a party boat with a few lively girls and some clerical looking personage who ate luncheon just like a common man. They were heading out for the lighthouse on Montauk Point with no idea when we'd be getting back. But those Long Island girls are as terraquesous as the men and beat me hollow in all matters connected with sailing. I blessed my lucky stars. But the Indians there are a degraded, shiftless and intemperate lot. Amazing they are not very thievish, considering their poverty. In fact, less so than any race of people I've known. But oh I was master of my time back than. Must be sad to see me now, eh boy? Back than I could make love in the divine word of Shakespeare himself until the tears ran down my lover's cheeks in great torrents. But then again I've never been a particularly sensibly behaved creature, have I boy?"

100

"Can't say that I know you well enough to make a judgment like that sir, seeing as I only just..."

Whitman went on in his reverie, not listening to the boy or even realizing his presence. He'd been that way his whole life, friendlier to folks in his writing than when they were standing right before him.

"Oh, it was a time to howl all right. My appetite was sharpened with a steely knife ready for the tender fat of life itself until the war caused my heart to collapse. And the word took over for my otherwise depressed animation. Anyway, it was time to pull up stakes. Night had come on all over the country and it was only the light of Lincoln that shone us through. But back then the only army I saw was the countless armies of heaven marching stilly in the space above as I fell asleep in a furled sail and headed home." Whitman closed his eyes and lapsed into the soft cushions of his memories, tilting his head back and imagining to breathe in the salted night air on the sea.

"I think you lost me sir. I was asking about my ma, if you remember."

Whitman looked perplexed, examined his palms and then bounced his head up.

"I was born in West Hills myself but still that's in the Township of Huntington. Use to visit the harbor often enough: silent, avoiding the moonbeams, blending myself in with the shadows."

"Excuse me sir?"

"Its from a poem son, just can't help myself. You know I use to have my own newspaper, The Long Islander. Bought a good horse and every week went round the country serving my papers - never had a happier jaunt. Heard old Elias Hicks preaching myself. Did you know they named Hicksville after the old prophet? Never sounded like too dignified a name for a town to me...but you said Huntington, eh?"

"Yes sir, Huntington. Wagram's Tavern was the place."

Then Whitman's face lit up: "The little girl in Wagram's tavern, of course! That was she and you're her son!" He pulled the boy and hugged him close, then held him at arm's length and stared at him intently. "And all is right in the universe, I suppose."

"Not in my universe I don't suppose," said Petit Jean perplexed.

"Didn't mean to be flippant son. Nothing worse than an old man rambling on, and a poet at that, eh?"

"I suppose."

"What happened to your pa? Was he a soldier? Fresh out of the army? Quite a few of them were hanging around that Tavern if I remember?"

"He's been killed, sir. Shot in a saloon out in old Oklahoma over a game of poker."

"To come through that god awful war and then...I don't suppose we're meant to make sense of the wretchedness on this place earth, are we, boy?"

"Don't suppose so, sir"

"Me, I ask no questions, boy, but eat thankfully. I advise you to do the same. You'll be amazed at the amount of vitality that resides in man, and woman too."

Petit Jean looked down at the floor. "My ma has gotten a taste for the liquor, sir."

"Don't let the tameness of respectable society get you down son. Although I've known many a fine drunk in my day - and perhaps your ma is one of them - I've always been a temperate man myself. Once wrote a novel called *Franklin Evans or The Inebriate* which was more to the point - about a Long Island lad be-deviled and besotted by drink until he sank lower and lower into vice and crime. At the end he takes the pledge. Don't suppose your ma has done that?"

"No sir, not to my knowledge she hasn't." Petit Jean looked up at the poet's kindly eyes. "Exactly what pledge you be referring to?"

"Not important, son, but that's the difference between novels and life. That's why I stopped writing them and put all my energies into living instead."

"And about my ma? What do you think I should do?"

"Not much you can do there, I imagine. I advise you to put your energies into celebrating yourself, son. Remember, first the man is shaped in the woman, but then he can be shaped in himself."

"Who said that?"

"Me. And that's it in a nutshell as far as I'm concerned." Whitman stared as the afternoon light shone on the boy's innocent face, still whiskerless and his sandy blond hair hung down over his forehead. "Tell me son, have you had any experience with women yet?"

Petit-Jean hesitated to tell the poet of the things he had seen and felt in the Bordello where he lived and worked. "Can't say that I have yet, sir."

"And with men or other boys?"

"Sir?"

Whitman looked at the boy for a long time. "Two things are certain here today."

"And what might those be sir?"

"That I'm too old and you're too young. So come, let's talk of poetry."

At the end of his visit, Whitman wrote a small missive for the boy to send back to his ma and he asked the boy to come back and see him again if he cared to. Petit Jean found it easy to talk to Whitman and when he left the poet embraced him in his arms and held him close while breathing in the smell of the boy's hair. And then he told him to stay out of the army whatever he did.

"It seems not of men but a lot of devils and butchers, butchering one another...I get almost frightened at the world."

.   "Guess I better be going and catch the wagon back to Hoboken."

"Up sails, then, and away!" Whitman yelled out the door, "Come again son – beautiful boys like you come so rarely!"

Petit Jean ran down Mickel street anxious not to miss the carriage that would take him back to the seemingly sane world of Uncle George's thirteen whores. Once seated in the carriage he opened the paper Whitman had given him, anxious to send it to his mother right away.

"There was a child went forth every day, and the first object he looked upon and received with wonder of pity or love or dread, that object he became, and that object became part of him for the day or a certain part of the day...or for many years or stretching cycles of years."

And at once Petit Jean knew that Walt Whitman had written this for him and so it stayed in his pocket for the rest of his life.

A year later when Captain Al had too much grog even for his own rather extended stomach and went out back of the house to relieve himself he found Qwing So and Petit Jean up against one another in the alley. Petit Jean had pinned Qwing So's arms outright for the girl at first had put up some kind of a feeble struggle, but now there was no strain between them and their mouths were locked together in a way rarely seen inside the four walls of the bordello.

Soon, when it became obvious to all thirteen whores what was going on between the two young lovebirds who met daily for their secret rendezvous next to the outhouse, they assigned themselves to be the courting queens of Petit Jean and Qwing So, none more so than Nell, who decided to prepare Qwing So for the ways of a man. Of course Petit Jean didn't know it, but he couldn't have asked for a better teacher for his future wife and he benefited from her lessons for years to come.

The status quo of New York City politics was essentially a big pot of public funds and crab-clawed politicians, all digging in for whatever they could pull out for themselves and the public be damned. Thus, the populist reform movement of the 1880's was gaining more and more momentum and it was only a matter of time before Uncle George began to feel unwelcome in more places than the local parish church. In fact it was explained to him by Chief Hordy, formerly a "gratis" client of O'Keefe's Emporium, that George's money would no longer guarantee him any kind of protection either at the precinct or city hall. The new powers that be were set on cleaning up The Tenderloin once and for all, the local Irish gangs having gaining too much political power with each arriving boat of new immigrants.

George could see the writing was on the wall: he and his girls would have to find a safer harbor to go about their business. He huffed and puffed for a few weeks but finally accepted the inevitable, figuring he couldn't fight the hypocritical ways of society anymore but he just might be able to stay a few territories ahead of them and loaded six of the girls into two wagons also packed with a chandelier, a large nude oil painting, heavy lace curtains and a standup piano - all the accoutrements needed for any self respecting whore house - and crossed the ferry to New Jersey, bound for the train at Pittsburgh which would take him and his crew out west where there were untapped desires as big as the wide open prairies themselves. All of "Georgie's girls" were free to cross the frontier with him and for those that didn't George gave each a hundred bucks and all their lingerie and nightgowns, knowing few would last too long on the streets of Manhattan before either syphilis or the law got them. Big Nell herself threatened to head on out for San Francisco alone where she heard of a three-story bordello with silk sheets. But when she heard rumors of newly arrived contingents of Chinese girls who were giving it away for almost nothing at all, just to find a husband, she fell back in with George, who was determined to bring the number of girls back to thirteen once he hit the wide open spaces, always figuring that to be a lucky number in an unlucky business.

Being the superstitious creature that Nell was, she was also put off by George's straight faced suggestion that the line of navigation of the genitals of the Chinese ladies ran the other way, somewhat akin to the slants of their eyes and it was only when Qwing So's three sisters agreed to strip and prove to Nell that their own flower stems ran in the same direction as hers, that they were not at all that different from the old girl herself (with the exception of their silky black puffs of pubic hair and full sets of teeth) that Nell was relieved enough to get on the ferry and begin the journey west.

Petit Jean was now not so little anymore. In the years he had been living in the bordello, playing by the Hudson River docks and watching his Uncle he had learned more about men and whoring and business than he might of during a lifetime on the prairie. He was a younger, thinner version of his Uncle George now, dressed in his own velvet suit and seemingly well adapted to his new lifestyle. Tips from the brothel had added up to a nice little bundle safely tucked away, and even with him now sending his ma a gold eagle form time to time, he still had enough to support his hopes of taking Antoinette and his mother off to California for a new life someday. Last time Uncle George had lined his back up straight against the outhouse door and took a knife to mark the spot, Petit Jean had grown to a man's size and George insisted that with feet as large as Petit Jean's he was bound to be a giant. He was wrong. For Petit Jean stayed at just 5'9" and never an inch more. But his face was a handsome combination of both his parents' heritage with his father's ready Irish smile and his mother's comely French features.

The question of where exactly Uncle George would set up shop for him and his girls was still unsettled. George, being no buckaroo and a man who liked his comforts, was appalled by the thought of going to some tent city, some last minute gold rush town with no running water or electricity. That was strictly out of the question. He was looking more for some kind of a frontier palace to set up his classy establishment, rather than a five minute rest home for lonely miners two years gone in the mountains, with a mandatory bath required for all clients. Texas was always a strong contender, with all that steer money floating around but George was reluctant to go where any unrepentant Confederates might still harbor a grudge against him. Finally he set his sights on Denver, Colorado, a thriving silver mining town in the northeast corner of the state. To make a respectable entrance into the community he planned on disguising his operation as a theater troupe, and once in Denver he even began putting on a highly edited and bastardized version of *Romeo and Juliet* in which Petit Jean was grudgingly forced into the male role on more than a few occasions, while Uncle George, of course, busily made side deals for any of his *actresses* who caught a horny theater-goers' eye.

Soon he found a saloon in Denver gone bust. The local madam had just overdosed on morphine and after an outrageous funeral attended by over two thousand devotees, folks - especially the men-folk - were wondering what was to become of her old haunt and were more than anxious for a replacement to open its doors, there being few available women west of the Mississippi. Within weeks, George O'Keefe had hung his own chandeliers and covered the walls with large nude paintings. Under his gold-framed voluptuous nudes, the piano was playing the popular songs of the day while his girls paraded up and down the short staircase in their fine New York lingerie. In less than a fortnight, business was booming and notorious personages of the west were making their way through O'Keefe's Saloon as if drawn to an oasis or a genuine fountain of youth.

Bob Ford sat in the corner table of O'Keefe's Emporium in Denver with his back to the door playing cards; he was a luckless player with no balls for bluffing or brains for cheating. With so many Missourians looking for an excuse to shoot him dead in the back as he had done to Jesse James, Bob didn't want to give anybody the opportunity to do the same. His brother Charley sat upstairs in the balcony with a shotgun at his side. Normally, George O'Keefe didn't allow weapons of any sort at all into the bar, but he made an exception for Bob and Charley Ford, hiring them for security and figuring that it would help keep peace in his establishment and prevent any of his girls from being damaged by a stray bullet. Besides, having as infamous a personage as Jesse James' assassin in your saloon didn't hurt business at all.

In fact Charley and Bob Ford were just killing time in Denver until they could put together a stash of cash and catch the stage for San Francisco where they were booked to present another of their "hair-raising" performances, reenacting the assassination of Jesse James. The performance was truthful enough and did not stray from the generally held belief that Jesse was shot in the back by a coward, while standing on a stool in his family home adjusting a picture frame. Jesse had trusted Bob and Charlie Ford; after all, they were recent members of his gang of thieves, even if his own brother Frank did have a funny feeling about the two. Bob Ford did not pretend to be a hero when he shot Jesse in the back, while the outlaw's long suffering wife Zoë fixed supper in the kitchen and their two small children played outside their modest home in St. Jo, Missouri. If anything, Bob Ford de-emphasized his own courage in his performance of the murder while boosting the chivalry of the Pinkerton Detectives who had offered him the reward. For some time after, the Ford brothers never slept at the same time, fearing that Jesse's brother Frank was coming after them. But shortly after Jesse's murder Frank himself surrendered in Missouri, stood trial and was declared innocent. Frank hung up his gums and declared his days of living outside the law over, retiring to his farm. Out west, the only problem the brothers ran into was with those miners so out of touch with the goings on of the world that they were under the impression that these brothers had something to do with the murder of Abraham Lincoln, as it was in "Ford's" theater that J.W. Booth did his own cowardly deed. Of course, the Ford brothers would have happily laid Abe in his grave, as well, them being as committed to the lost rebel cause as Jesse had been himself.

Their short performance, which they had repeated in Denver until the whole town had seen it at least twice, consisted of Charlie Ford imitating Jesse himself, wearing a false beard and strapping on replicas of Jesse's signature double shoulder holsters and two Remington revolvers. The only problem was that Bob often forgot his own lines, a retelling of the Northfield, Minnesota bank robbery where Jesse had lost half his gang including the murderous Younger brothers. Bob and Charlie thanked their lucky stars that all of the Youngers were either in jail or graves, them being hotheads and more likely to seek revenge then even Frank James. The actual reenactment of the killing itself was often greeted with cheers as well as boos. Jesse James was nobody's real enemy, just a clever thief and ex-Rebel who learned his murderous trade while still in his teens riding with Quantrill's raiders and participating in the bloody attack on Lawrence, Kansas where all Union supporters, including women and children, were summarily executed. History, however, would credit him as being the first outlaw to successful rob a moving train. Charlie would play

111

Jesse standing on the chair, arranging a framed "Home Sweet Home" embroidery while Bob snuck up behind him and held his revolver, loaded with smoky blanks right at his back. The boos didn't really bother Bob Ford so much; he had never dreamed of being a hero, only a legend. He was a squirrelly kind of fellow with big owl eyes and it was only poor Jesse's notorious lack of character judgment and the lack of available help that allowed the Ford brothers to enter his gang at that late stage anyway. Towards the end, like any king with a host of enemies, Jesse James tended to surround himself with anyone who would listen to past tales of glory, bragging of being a professional bank and train robber for over fifteen years and never spending a day in jail. But life had gotten too peaceful in St. Joseph Missouri for a man like him, living a docile family life while masquerading as a cattle broker named "Mr. Howard." And even if Bob Ford had not gotten him, chances are he would soon have been caught or killed while attempting to pull off another of his megalomaniac schemes, like the debacle of the Northfield, Minnesota raid, and ending his days ignominiously in prison or propped up dead on a wood plank in front of a sheriff's office. Jesse James had died a legend, which was just what he had always wanted and he could thank Bob Ford for that.

Petit Jean had heard little of Jesse James before he started reading the dime novels written by Ned Buntline that were popular back east. Uncle George was keen on teaching the boy how to read and, as he already knew his letters, it was not a tough job. He was hungry to learn and in the afternoons, those whores who could read would help him with his

112

spelling, and soon he was beyond the pulp fiction of Ned Buntline and even diving into *Ivanhoe*.

It was Barbara Banner, the mayor's favorite, who had given Petit Jean his own copy of Walt Whitman's "Leaves of Grass" for his birthday back in New York. In his room Petit Jean would peer at the pages for hours, understanding little but sure there was magic in those words that might pull his family back together again. But at the same time the book had confused Petit Jean: where was the story, the action, the plot?

"But Miss Banner?" he had demanded of her one afternoon. "Just who is the hero in this here Whitman book? There ain't no Hickok or Buffalo Bill or Jesse James – just himself."

Barbara looked at him smiling. "That's the point lil' Jean," she said in her soft Georgia accent. "The hero is you and the hero is him. And the book is a celebration of this miraculous world we live in spite of all the cruelty and barbarity around us." She opened to the first page. "See here lil' Jean, 'I celebrate myself, and what I assume you shall assume. For every atom belonging to me as good belongs to you...' Now you see what I mean, he's talking about you and him together."

"But he never met me before he wrote the book," said Petit Jean, "My ma says she met him but that was before I was born. I promise you that."

"He don't need to have met you," said Barbara. "Because he figures you're just the same as him even if he never set his eyes on you."

Petit Jean had held the book in his hands and looked at the grainy photo of the gray haired man with sad eyes looking away somewhere, with his white shirt rakishly open at the collar. "He sure don't look like me," he said.

Barbara laughed. "It don't matter what he looks like. His words say that his soul looks like yours and I reckon that's true, sugar."

"Is there a picture of that thing...a soul?"

"No, I don't believe there exists a picture of a true soul in the whole wide world. I imagine its something like the air we breathe - it just exists somewhere and we know it without ever having to see it."

Petit Jean held the book and read the first three lines again. "Just one other thing Miss Banner, what's an atom?"

This question stumped her. "I'm not sure...but I think its what our insides is made up of. I'll have to ask the Mayor on that one next time he comes by. He'll come up with some crazy answer if he knows it or not!"

Petit Jean was sad when Barbara Banner did not accompany Uncle George out West but with the whorehouse closed down, the mayor had set her up in her own apartment in Chelsea, with a discreet back entrance for his continuing nightly visits.

Chapter 9

Even though being in Denver put him closer to their part of the world, Petit Jean had stopped receiving letters from anyone in Vendee, be it his ma or Father Bachet. So while George O'Keefe continued setting up his Bordello to his satisfaction, Petit Jean put together all the money he had been saving and booked himself a seat on the Kansas Pacific Railroad that would take him from Denver over to Topeka, Kansas, where he might rent a horse and ride down to Vendee.

When Petit Jean arrived in Vendee some weeks later, the first thing he did was walk behind the Catholic Church and stand for some minutes over his father's grave. The crude wooden cross that was planted there had started to deteriorate and white paint flakes lay around it. He heard the bells ringing from the Baptist chapel down the street and then the dark shadow of Father Bachet came across the face of the cross. Petit Jean nearly tripped over the rocks covering his father's grave as he spun around to see the priest standing behind him, his hands folded in front of his long black habit, his eyes intense, his cruel mouth smiling terribly.

"The prodigal son returns," said Father Bachet.

'The what?" said Petit Jean.

"You've come back, son," said Father Bachet.

"Suppose I have at that," said Petit Jean. "My Uncle moved his, uh...restaurant, out to Denver and I been living up there. Came back to see my ma and sister...can you help me locate either of them?"

"Did you really think this was such a wise idea, son? To just show up unannounced without warning? Without even taking the time to write us first and let us know your plans? You know, to suddenly appear could be a great shock to your mother's delicate condition."

"I didn't think about that father...I just wanted to see my ma and sister again. Besides, I haven't no letters in a long time."

"That's because your mother has gone away."

"What do you mean?" asked Jean in a panic. "Gone where?"

"She went away with Judge Durand right after the wedding."

"Who's wedding?"

"Their own wedding. She is currently traveling with Judge Durand who has pressing business elsewhere in the territory. They are legally married now and you'll have to respect the Judge as your stepfather and try to put the past behind you."

"Like hell I will," said Petit Jean defiantly.

"God will not allow a child to come between a husband and wife who have taken their vows before our savior."

Petit Jean said nothing. His eyes narrowed and his heart filled with pain and rage.

"Then at least I'm going to take my sister with me back to Denver," he said finally. "She can stay with me and Uncle George. I'll take care of her."

"I'm afraid that will be impossible. You see, Antoinette has run off some time ago. It nearly broke your mother's heart. I tried to instill the

116

love of Jesus within her soul but she refused to obey the law of the church and so I told her she must leave. I have no idea where she is now. As far as the church is concerned she is...forever lost."

"You're lying! You ain't no man of God. You're as sinful as that damn Judge Durand. My mother never woulda married such a man. I'm sure of that."

"You had better go now son. I think the liberal ways back east have distorted your thinking."

"I'll be back."

"We all will," said Father Bachet. "Back to our maker."

A crude sign now fronted the Vendee saloon but the interior had changed little since the last time Petit Jean was there on that terrible day. The same poker table, same rickety chairs gathered around it. He went to the bar and ordered a lemonade and didn't hear the Indian walk in, but next time he looked over at the coal-burning stove, there he was, sitting with his arms crossed, saying nothing. Petit Jean walked over to him.

"You were there weren't you?" He asked and Jack Blankets, dressed in buckskins and the torso of a blue cavalry jacket, seemed to grunt an affirmative reply.

"I know you was there," said Petit Jean. He drew close to the Indian's ear. "I'm going to kill Judge Durand myself someday," he said. "You can be sure of that."

"He kill you first," said Indian Jack. "Just like your father."

"What?" Said Petit Jean. "Why, I'll shoot that bastard before..."

117

"You no shooter," interrupted the Indian. "Me, I'm shooter, know many things."

"Like what?"

"Like what Oklahoma mean to begin with."

"Mean nothing far as I know - just is."

"Mean Red People - Okla mean people in Choctaw, Humma mean red. All these Indian haters living in territory of red people."

"Teach me to shoot then," said Petit Jean jokingly. "If you know so damn much."

"I'm here for that," said Jack Blankets seriously. "Bet your life on it, boy."

"But if you know I'm going to kill Durand and Carpis too, why do you want to help me?"

"Durand is evil bastard, too evil to live. Carpis is like rat, make everything dirty around him. Best to kill both."

"So why don't you kill them yourself if you feel so strongly about it?"

"If I kill them, they hang me quick from nearest tree. No trial. Just one more dead Indian. You kill them and maybe you get killed too but no one gonna hang you so quick."

In the weeks that followed the Indian hardly spoke to Petit Jean except when absolutely necessary. He was talkative enough when he came across one of his own people but Petit Jean just figured he had nothing to say of importance to him, a white boy, who understood nothing of the way of the wind and the moon and coyotes. When the Indian did find

118

words for the boy, he would blurt them out quickly, not looking at him. But the main thing he did needed no words at all: he just kept teaching the boy how to shoot a gun until he did it well enough to stand a chance against Durand and Carpis.

On the day of his first shooting lesson, the Indian showed up at the now deserted old O'Keefe farm, where Petit Jean was waiting. He dragged a rusted plate of chest armor behind him and built a small fire, carefully making two-dozen red, green and yellow wax bullets from a brass mold. Then from out of his saddlebags Jack Blankets drew a gleaming pair of Remington 44 pistols and gave them to Petit Jean.

"These come from Jesse James," said the Indian. "These guns know how to kill a man real good - have plenty of practice, these guns. Man stay killed with these guns. No getting up after."

"I met the man who killed him back in Denver, use to put on a play about it. Never dreamed I'd be using the same guns as Jesse James."

"Don't dream," said Jack Blankets. "Just shoot."

The Remington 44's were old-fashioned guns with a single action making it necessary to cock the hammer back before pulling the trigger. The Indian said that Jesse James himself had worked on the pistols and brought the trigger back a few hairs more with a fine metal file so the guns could be fanned and shot in one motion. He taught Petit Jean to fan the hammer with the trigger already cocked as the gun left his holster, using his wrist as the swivel point and aiming from his hip, never taking his eye off his target.

"Aim for the chest," said the Indian. "You aim for head you probably miss – white man's brain too little. You shoot man in right arm - he still have left arm. Shoot him in the stomach, maybe he shoot you back and you both die. But shoot a man in his heart and spirit leave fast."

For days Petit Jean practiced the fast draw and wrist swivel and fanning and firing the two heavy pistols. Then Jack Blankets reloaded the two Remingtons with the wax slugs he had made in the brass cast and handed Petit Jean the two pistols while he struggled into the metal chest armor and stood about twenty-five yards from Petit Jean, whooping and waving his own gun in the air as if to be firing back at him. This all struck Petit Jean as kind of funny and he began giggling so the Indian let go a few live rounds that scattered the dust around the boy's feet.

"I got better things to do than teach a white boy to kill white men," griped the Indian. "There was nothing I could do when your father get killed and I lose some honor so now I do this for his son, win back some. But maybe I forget about honor if you think so damn funny."

"Sorry," said Petit Jean. "I appreciate what you're doing."

When Jack Blankets took his place again Petit Jean began carefully drawing and fanning the wax slugs off at the armor with as much accuracy as he could. After both pistols were empty they carefully examined the suit of armor for the red, green and yellow splotches of wax. Petit Jean had hit his mark with a few yellow slugs and was feeling pretty proud of himself but the Indian said he always loaded the first two chambers with red wax followed by the green and yellow, saying that the first two shots

120

more often than not decided which man was going to walk away alive. Very few men, even the best of shooters, could get more than two shots off before the other man, even a wounded man, had his own opportunity to fire back.

"Sometimes man gets lucky," said the Indian. "Kill you dead with third shot. You think you win fight and next thing you know - you know nothing. You dead, spirit gone. First law: don't stop shooting 'til you sure man stop moving. Next law: never turn your back on a wounded man."

The Indian did not wear a holster and no visible weapons but a long sheathed Bowie Knife. Petit Jean asked him why, "White men find out that an Indian can shoot this good they kill him, for sure."

When Petit Jean rode through the gates up to Edward Filloux's barn, the farmer barely recognized him from the boy he had last seen years before. Petit Jean could see the look of anxiety across Filloux's face, not knowing who was approaching him and probably deciding if he should extend a hand in greeting or a shotgun in warning.

"It's Petit Jean O'Keefe," he yelled from his horse when he got within hearing range.

"Oh blazes! It's you, boy. With the way things are going in this territory I didn't know whom to expect. There's a lot of rustler's about with the hard times and all these boomers killing each other over land claims."

"My daddy didn't raise me to be a rustler," said Petit Jean as he dismounted."

Like two farmers they chewed the fat on the weather and the price of cattle and pigs in that laconic way, as if they talked to each other every day, neither man looking the other in the eye, just fiddling with a piece of straw or stabbing their toe in the dirt. Finally Jean got around to what he was aiming at.

"What do you hear about my ma and my sister?"

"Don't hear much and what I do ain't good."

"Tell me," said Petit Jean.

"Guess you're old enough," said Filloux. "Well, your ma was gonna lose the farm to the bank anyway, so when Durand made her an offer, and believe me it weren't much, I guess she figured it was better then nothing so she sold the land to him although he ain't done a damn thing with it. Just let it rot, in my opinion. Had some rebels bivouacked out there for a while but they seem to have moved on. Then that priest, Father Bachet, brought them both to live in the church and he had your sister scrubbing the floors while Durand started sniffing around, courting your ma of all things. Seems your ma forgave the man who killed your father a little too quick, if you ask me, although I can say she was rarely in any state to decide about much of anything, not to mention getting hitched to the man who shot her husband."

"You mean my mom really married Durand? I can't believe it," He felt like his legs would crumble underneath him. "Such a thing can't be true...she would have written me first...she would have..."

"To be honest boy, she took such a liking to the liquor, couldn't get

122

enough of it. Don't reckon she was sober enough to know who she was marrying when she said *I do* in front of that priest."

Petit Jean couldn't speak, couldn't move. Finally Filloux began to talk of cyclones while the boy stood there trembling.

He found Antoinette some three months later after circling the Oklahoma territory, going down into Texas twice and far north into Nebraska before hearing a disquieting story about a crazy young whore who called herself Queen Antoinette and lived in the tent city of Perry, Oklahoma: a place referred to by all as *Hell's Half Acre*. The cowboy who he heard the story from said the whore was surely deranged and imagined herself to be some kind of a French queen in an invented kingdom but he was sure she called herself Antoinette And Petit Jean wondered how many Antoinette's there could be in Oklahoma.

He entered Perry early one morning and Hells Half Acre was already alive with piano music already coming out of the saloon. When he walked in he saw his sister sitting by herself at the bar, the sole customer as the bartender swatted flies and leaned on the player piano. From the sorry state of her dress it appeared as if she hadn't yet left the saloon from the night before or from many nights before that.

No longer a little girl dragging a doll behind her, Antoinette was now a budding teenager with her mother's flowing red hair. Her apperance was tattered and dirty with a powdered pink face as hard as any whore Petit Jean had ever seen. Any trace of a child's innocent smile had been lost to a painful whiskey grimace. Her red-checkered dress was torn at her knees and stained, her hair piled loosely on top of her head, uncombed and two circles of bright red rouge were painted doll-like on her pale cheeks. As Petit Jean beheld this pathetic apparition, he still could see his precious little sister, the same girl he use to play jacks with, and he longed to hold her and take care of her like his father surely would have wanted.

Petit Jean walked gingerly behind her.

"Antoinette?" He asked softly.

She swung around and tried to clobber him with her fist.

"Who has the nerve to disturb the queen at this ungodly hour?" she roared back. "Upon whose authority?"

She was clearly drunk and probably mad as well judging by the terrorized look in her eyes. She stared at Petit Jean but did not seem to recognize who he was.

"Antoinette, it's me, your brother Petit Jean. Don't you know me? Come on, say you know who I am and give a kiss and let's be out of this here hell hole, *ma petite soeur*."

"Petit Jean?" She called over to the bartender. "Does the queen have any brother by that name? Or is this more treachery by Cardinal Richelieu?"

"Come on, Antoinette. Mama needs you. I can buy you some new clothes and bring you back to Vendee, if you want. Or you can come along with me back to Uncle George's place in Denver, Colorado."

Antoinette said nothing. And than she spit at him. She tore the sleeve

124

of her filthy blouse and pushed her shoulder in his face showing the ripples of raised scars there. "I ain't never going back to Vendee and you can tell that priest that if he ever tries to whip me again I swear I'll kill him. How dare he strike the queen?" She downed her glass of whiskey and began to sing loudly in French.

That afternoon, after hours of futile pleading for her to come with him, Petit Jean mounted his horse and rode out of Perry alone. He had left his sister Antoinette sitting on a muddy *throne* in the gutter from which she had refused to move. He had talked to her for hours but she never did say a sane word and he finally just gave up. Petit Jean figured that both his mama and now his sister were forever gone to worlds of drunkenness and madness that he couldn't bring them back from with his own unaided strength. His family was blown to hell and he knew there was no way he could fix it, no way that he could undo *God's will*, in the words of Father Bachet. But he no longer believed in any God whose will could be so cruel.

Passing the small farms on the trail out of Perry, he thought of his pa John O'Keefe and how the sun had shone off his freckled, smiling face as he once held Petit Jean high up in the air while his ma called them all in for dinner, holding the boy's back to the sunset and proclaiming, "Petit Jean, the whole world be talking about you someday!"

Petit Jean wept for a moment before spurring his horse west on the trail to Colorado. Jack Blankets had taught him how to kill and now Antoinette had given him one more reason to do it. He knew that one day

125

he would surely kill Judge Durand and Carpis but now he had a feeling that there would be a long line of dead men leading up to that moment, for it would take more than two dead men to satisfy his lust for revenge. Antoinette had taught him to forget everything about reason and decency and he was afraid of no man now and his anger burnt cold and constant in his chest, on another plane, invisible to all.

It took a while - years in fact – for Petit Jean to utilize all that the Indian taught him. He practiced for sure, day in and day out, and spent hours just outside of Denver shooting, fighting deadly duels with scrub-brush and cactus but no man had yet tested him. He continued to work in his Uncle's new *O'Keefe's Emporium*, stocking the bar, tending to the laundry, flirting with Qwing So and more, but still he was the boy of the place who would run and get something when you needed it. Not quite in short pants but certainly not yet a man.

The west was a huge frontier, larger then most European countries, but the number of boomtowns visited by badmen on a regular basis was limited and predictable: St. Louis, Dodge City, Tombstone, Deadwood, Denver and farther west, to San Francisco. Situated fairly equidistant between Mexico, Canada, the Pacific Coast and the law-abiding East, Denver held a geographic advantage as well as the must-see attractions of imany shiny saloons and at least one gentrified bordello full of genuine New York whores. So of course Denver was among the first stops for any desperado with money to spend.

George O'Keefe had handled his share of tough drunken sailors back on Canal Street where most of them were unarmed and easily subdued, but out west most men carried arms and seemed inclined to use them if necessary. The only posted rule of his place was that anyone drawing a pistol during a card game would be immediately ejected from the premises, although exactly how that was to be enforced nobody knew as of yet.

It was a Sunday afternoon, and *O'Keefe's Emporium* was packed with cowboys and those non-church going citizens who preferred a bottle of whisky to a bottled up sermon in one of the local houses of worship. There were five card games going on and the girls sashayed from table to table, ready to show a winner a lucrative (for the girls, that is) time upstairs in one of their private rooms. Cum and Qwik were standing behind a driver named Lanahan who had just come off a silver run from Fort Collins, hauling the precious ore behind a team of 6 horses. A big and powerful man, who never took off his mutilated droopy hat, Lanahan was no stranger to *O'Keefe's* and had never caused trouble but suddenly, he stood up out of his chair and grabbed each of the girls by the throat.

"You chinks bringing me bad luck!"

"Please mister," cried Cum. "We bring good luck. You come upstairs, we show you."

"You're two godless chink whores," he cried. "Get away from me." And he threw the two girls back onto the table behind him, Qwik hitting the floor so hard that she passed out. George O'Keefe was running quick from behind the bar with a leather blackjack in his hand but as he

127

approached Lanahan form the back, the driver swung around and George found himself looking down the barrel of a long barreled Colt 45.

"You want some of this?' said Lanahan menacingly. "Well then, come and get it."

"We don't want no trouble here," said George O'Keefe. "But you can't be manhandling my girls like that. They ain't done nothing to you."

"I do what I like with them two godless chink whores and no New York mick gonna tell me different."

"Why don't you take what's yours off that table and walk out of here," said George O'Keefe. "As you can see I'm not carrying a gun and no gunplay will be tolerated in here."

Petit Jean stood at the top of the balcony with arms full of laundry, transfixed, watching the scene below him. Silently, he put down the laundry and went back to his room and from out of his chest he took two single holsters and crisscrossed them around his waist with the Remington 44's swung low across his hips. He checked the loaded cylinders of each pistol and spun them on his finger before slipping them back in the holsters. He spit on his hand and slicked the blond forelock that nearly hung over his eyes back behind his ear and put on the black deerskin gloves that fit like a second skin and prevented any sweat from loosening his grip on the pistols. Within a minute he was back at the balcony, his hand resting loosely on the pearl handles of the two Remingtons.

"Hey mister," he said as he walked down the stairs into the barroom. "My uncle he don't wear a gun, never has far as I know, so why don't you just do like he says and leave this place right quick."

Everyone in the barroom including George O'Keefe, all the whores and Lanahan himself were now staring in amazement at the boy descending the stairs with the big guns on his waist.

"Son, I suggest you stay out of this unless you want me to pull down your pants and give you a whooping right here and now." Laughed Lanahan. "In fact, I suppose I might enjoy that." He started walking towards the boy with his long-barreled Colt at his side.

"Petit Jean, " said his Uncle, "You stay out of this and get back upstairs. I can take care of this fool by myself, boy."

"Who you calling a fool?" said Lanahan and he swung around and shot George O'Keefe in the leg. "Now boy, you get over here and pull your trousers down and I'm gonna give you a whooping. Or else I'm gonna shoot your butt right full of lead!"

But when Petit Jean came to the bottom of the stairs he just smiled. "Mister, I suggest you get *your* big fat ass out of this place before I shoot it out from under you. And you can leave your money on the table. And somebody fetch a doctor for my Uncle right away! And you, you bastard, you caused enough trouble for today."

Petit Jean wanted this over fast, he knew his anger was both his greatest weapon and his Achilles heel, and since the murder of his father, his own fury had cooled to that of dry ice, coolly burning in the back of his mind and never about to let him go off half cocked, taking chances he might regret or be caught with nothing but a wooden pistol to defend himself. And most important, he wouldn't make the same mistake as his daddy. In a situation like this he knew screaming words showed a man at his greatest emotional weakness - his most vulnerable side. In the few gunfights he had seen in Denver, more times than not, it was the screaming braggart, boasting of how he was going to kill this one or that, who ended up moaning on the floor with a belly full of lead. In the west, it was more often the quiet men who won the fights, men like Hickok whose one fatal mistake was the time he sat with his back to the door or the cold-blooded Texan *shootist*, John Wesley Harding, who once killed a man for snoring too loud.

Petit Jean walked slowly over to the bar, not taking his eyes of Lanahan, and took a mouth full of whiskey.

"That's right, boy. You're gonna need a drink after I'm through with you, you little..."

He walked over to Lanahan and spat out the whiskey hard on the man's face. As Lanahan reached with his free hand to wipe the alcohol from his eyes Petit Jean pulled out one of his Remington's and fanned five shots into Lanahan's chest at close range. Lanahan fell back over a chair, his gun firing wildly into the ceiling. Petit Jean leaned down over Lanahan, his foul stained shirt still smoking from the strength of the blasts and pulled Lanahan's own Bowie knife out of its scabbard and chopped off the man's trigger finger, wrapping it in a Queen of Spades lying on the table. Then he threw the bloody package into the air and put three bullets right through it with his other Remington before it hit the ground.

The bar was in total silence and Petit Jean looked around him. His Uncle George was sitting flat out on the floor his hands clamped around the fleshy part of his thigh where the bullet had grazed him.

"I…uh…well, I guess that man didn't need his trigger finger no more anyway," said Petit Jean, putting his guns away, walking up the stairs to the balcony and retrieving the scattered laundry he had been holding.

But he didn't take off his guns, and now Petit Jean knew that he would always be wearing the low black holsters with the Remingtons so he could fan his palm across the hammer just as he swiveled the gun forward. He was nearly as fast and accurate as the Indian Jack Blankets himself, but after killing Lanahan he was confident enough to know that if he stood in the street at high noon face to face with any man, his chances were better than even.

He was surprised at the quiet that had settled upon him after Lanahan lay dead on the floor. It was a good feeling, a feeling of peace and he felt nothing for the dead man; not guilt or even the slightest sense of remorse. In fact, he felt better. In a strange way, killing that man had given his life some sort of direction, meaning and motivation. He supposed that he could kill men like Lanahan all day long, no problem at all.

Uncle George had watched the whole thing from where he sat on the floor wounded; he had never even seen Petit Jean shoot a pistol before, much less cut off a dead man's finger. He sat transfixed, open mouthed, not knowing what to say until finally he blurted out over the bar's hushed silence:

"My dear nephew, you don't seem so 'petit' anymore to me." And then the barroom exploded with laughter and the piano player started playing a merry tune and two miners dragged the body of Lanahan, leaving a bloody trail behind it, outside into the gutter where the horses waited silently.

PART TWO: JOHN LITTLE

Guthrie, Oklahoma 1893

Chapter 10

Jonathan A. Hoades, president of the Statehood Bank in Guthrie, Oklahoma, walked briskly across the forever muddy and ineptly named Chicago Avenue that ran in front of his cherished bank. It was still early morning and he hoped no one would see him as he headed toward the telegraph shack located in back of the Atchison Topeka & Santa Fe Railway depot. Held in his hand was a short message he had written out in his own hand to be wired to a Mr. John Little c/o O'Keefe's Emporium, Denver, Colorado.

While the telegraph operator tapped out the message, Hoades took a deep breath, pulling out his monogrammed handkerchief to wipe the nervous perspiration from his brow. He never imagined finding himself in such an awkward and precarious position: he, the president of the town's bank and a pillar of the community, reaching out for help to a known killer. Of course, reliable sources had assured him that John Little was one of the most credible paid-for-hire gunman to be found in the west and still, it was in the bank's - and therefore the town's - best interest to hire such a man, or so he tried to make himself believe. Hoades was a conservative and outwardly religious man and a very prudent banker whose cautious nature would normally forbid him to take such radical steps, to enter into such a risky proposition. After all, this gunman John Little, this so-called regularizer, was a man whom he had never even set eyes on, and, in fact, he knew him only from his lethal and widespread reputation. His anxiety ran wild. What was to keep a man like this from just as easily using his deadly skills to run off with a hefty share of the bank's precious assets for himself? And then who would there be to protect the bank if things went wrong like that?

As he entered the telegraph shack Hoades decided that the blame for his troubles laid right square on the head of the local lawman. If he had any kind of faith in the Federal Marshall, whose job it was to dispense law and order throughout the new territory, then he wouldn't be wiring a man like John Little in the first place.

"But now with the army gone further west up against the Sioux, there's no one else but this man Little who folks say can surely guarantee results," the banker whispered to himself as the old telegraph operator leaned over and tapped out his message - dots and dashes - on the brass telegraph key.

"Or guarantee that this John Little won't lay you six feet under as well!" The telegraph operator added chuckling. Embarrassed that he had been voicing his anxieties out loud, the bank president cleared his throat.

"This is purely confidential, you understand. I don't want to hear no gossip being passed around town here. This is a matter of security for us all, you understand?"

"My lips are sealed like an envelope," said the telegraph operator.

Ten days following the dispatch of the telegram, John Little finally rode into Guthrie after circling the town for some hours or so before entering, first studying all the possibilities of an ambush through the sights of his Sharps buffalo rifle. Finally, convinced all was clear, he had spurred his horse and trotted quickly through the main road into town, looking from left to right until finally steering his horse into the corral of the livery stable at the end of the street. Slowly dismounting, he took off his long canvas duster, laying it across the saddle of his big bay and patting the horse's rump while keeping the other hand on the pistol in his belt; carefully he looked around the corral for any immediate trouble that might be coming his way. More than once he had found himself the target of some half baked ambush before even getting into the town proper, but since then his habit of taking a series of roundabout entries had left more than a few would be bushwhackers lying dead behind rocks, stiff fingers still gripping Winchester rifles, tongues swelling in the sun. John Little refused to bury such men.

The liveryman stood at the stable entrance, chewing on a long piece of straw, and watching John Little as he swung his saddlebags off the haunches of his horse that shifted the weight on his hindquarters and swatted flies with his tail.

"Fine looking horse," said the liveryman. "If you got a mind to sell him, I got a mind to buy him."

"This filly is not for sale," said John Little. "Sentimental reasons, you understand."

"I can understand that, mister. You must be a cattleman, I reckon."

"Can't say that I am."

"You be with the railroads then?" asked the stable owner. "Come to survey where they'll be laying the rails for that new line heading out to California?"

John Little showed no expression. "I'm no railroad man." But with his tailored dark suit, string tie and high boots, the stable owner couldn't figure out what else a man dressed in such a fashion might be.

"Don't mean to be prying into a man's business, mind you. But I just kind of figured with that long gunny sack tied across your saddle horn there - well I reckon its probably some kind of telescope or surveying instrument, what not. You know, making sure them Chinaman lay them rails straight."

"Got something against Chinamen? "

John Little untied the long canvas sack from his saddle and opened it up for the liveryman to see: it was a gleaming Sharps buffalo rifle with brass fittings, an extended barrel and a fancy adjustable sight the likes of which the liveryman had never seen before. "I suppose this might be what you're interested in looking at, *monsieur?*"

The stable man looked down at the gleaming weapon and than up to John Little. "Ain't never seen a railroad man carrying no rifle like that," he said in surprise.

"Reckon not," said John Little. "Take fine care of my horse there will you. Give her plenty of oats. Been a long journey for both of us."

"Yes sir," said the stable man. "Don't worry none, that bay of yours will be well cared for in my stable. You can be assured of that, sir, because..."

John Little began to walk away, his saddlebags slung over his shoulder when the liveryman suddenly cursed to himself, "God damn me if I ain't some kind of blasted fool!" He called out after him with a shout:

"Why...are you that man Little? The man-killer the bank wired? I should have known it was you - carrying a weapon like that."

John Little turned around and eyed the man, cocking his head, and checking the man's attitude for any sign of belligerence but finding none. He broke into a grin. "Man-killer? I suppose that would be me after all, monsieur," he said and continued to walk away. Then he stopped in the doorway of the stable and turned slowly, staring at the liveryman. "I answered your question, now you answer mine."

"What be that...sir?"

"What you got against the Chinese?"

"Why...nothing, I suppose."

"That's the right answer. My wife is Chinese. I'd hate to think you might be insulting her good people."

The liveryman gulped hard. "Didn't mean any offence, mister."

"None taken," said John Little who continued crossing the street content to have scared the hell out of another fool.

The liveryman took the horse by his studded black bridal and walked him across the corral, reckoning he better scrape the big bay's hooves out very carefully just in case this man Little might be as touchy about his horse as he was about his wife. Wouldn't want a man like that to come back and be cross with you, thought the liveryman, as he gently led the horse inside the dark stable.

John Little crossed the dusty street, now busy with the midday traffic of wagons, horses and riders, and climbed up on a newly built raised wooden sidewalk - a sure sign of the creeping refinement that had entered the former Indian Territory with the first land rush. He entered the bank, stood for a moment trying to figure out where the whirring noise was coming from and than looked upward to see a swirling ventilator fan rotating from the ceiling.

From in back of one of the barred teller booths came a squeaky voice. "Runs on Kerosene. Mr. Hoades says the next closest bank with a contraption like that is all the way out in San Francisco."

"I'll take his word on that," said John Little. "And you can go tell your patron that John Little has come to say Bon Jour."

The teller's eyes went wide as he stared at John Little, momentarily paralyzed before spinning around and bursting right into the office of Mr. Jonathan Hoades, Bank President, even forgetting to knock as he normally would. After all, wasn't this the day the whole town had been waiting for since Mr. Hoades had sent that telegram just over a week ago?

"Sir, he's here sir! He's standing right outside my teller window looking up at that contraption on the ceiling!" He announced loudly.

"What in blazes are you yelling about Milroy? Can't you see I'm in a conference here?" The harried teller took a long look around and lowered his voice after realizing that the bank president was smoking cigars with a

139

few of the other town notables: a cattleman and the saloon owner. Milroy apologized, "Oh yes sir...I'm sorry sir," and walked back out of the office to begin knocking timidly on the bank president's open door.

"For God's sake get back in here Milroy!" yelled Hoades.

"Yes sir?" Said Milroy.

"I suppose you mean to say that this man John Little has arrived in Guthrie? This man I sent a *confidential* telegram to a short time ago?"

Hoades' cohorts smirked among themselves.

"Might as well put a sign in the window next time, Jonathan," said the cattleman.

"Yes sir, Mr. Hoades," said Milroy. "That would be him just outside, this man Little. Although I can't say he looks like much of a killer," said the teller. "Looks more like some kind of East Coast dandy if you asked me."

"Have you ever seen a killer before, Milroy?" Asked Hoades.

"Well...I seen a picture or two of the James boys," said the teller.

"Never mind that. You just go back out there and you can tell Mr. Little that there's a room set up for him at the hotel where he can settle down and wash up after his long journey. And tell him I'll come by in an hour or so." Hoades, who had never actually seen a killer either, was wondering if he should let a few of his friends tag along with him to see this man John Little or if a one man welcoming committee might be more discrete.

"Care to join me?" he asked his friends but neither man replied.

140

The teller quickly relayed the message to John Little who nodded his head coolly in reply but said nothing. With his saddlebags slung over his shoulders and the long rifle cradled in his arms, he headed for the Crystal Hotel just down a bit on Chicago Street.

The best room in the hotel had indeed been prepared for him and once inside he laid his saddlebags on the bed and waited for the hotel boy to bring up some hot bath water. Once that was done he brought the saddlebags with him into the bathroom, stripped off his clothes and with a pleasurable sigh slid into the soothing water. Careful not to get his hands wet, he reached over the side of the tub into one of the saddle bags and pulled out two things most precious to him: a book and his gun. The loaded Remington he cocked and lay on a chair next to the tub and the book, a collection of verse by Walt Whitman, he carefully held in front of him while soaking in the tub. It was a well-thumbed volume to be sure, but John Little never grew tired of Whitman's words, his discovery of himself, his celebration of life. And it was as good a way as any to pass the time while waiting for the shooting and killing to begin.

After bathing, he carefully brushed off his suit, shined his boots and sat in a corner chair facing the door, fully dressed and continuing to read Walt Whitman, his Remington joining its sister back in his double shoulder holster, crisscrossed across his chest now.

'Is today nothing? Is the beginning less past nothing?' John Little read aloud. He was silently reflecting on those words when a creaking floorboard outside his door had him lay the book down across the bed and slowly

stand up while drawing both pistols in his hands. He held the gleaming guns straight out in front of him, holding his breath and counting ten heart beats, as was his custom before saying in a soft voice:

"If I were you, I'd swing that door open with your foot and stand there with your hands on your heads before I commence blasting away avec *mes deux pistolets la.*"

The door creaked slowly open, and standing with his hands over his head and a heavy line of sweat across his brow was Jonathan Hoades, the bank president.

"Don't shoot me, Mr. Little. For god's sake don't shoot me - I'm the man who sent you the telegram! I'm Jonathan Hoades, president of the bank here."

John Little uncocked his pistols and laid them across his legs. "You've a funny way of entering a man's room, Mr. Hoades. Standing outside my door like that without knocking."

"Well, I heard you talking to somebody in here and I didn't want to disturb..." Hoades looked in the room to see it was empty. "At least, I thought I heard you talking."

"Just with my muse, sir," chuckled John Little.

"Your...? Oh...well anyway, I was trying to figure out what the hell I was going to say myself, if you must know." He nervously giggled, "I hadn't entirely organized my thoughts for our meeting so I..."

"You can put your arms down if it be uncomfortable for you, sir."

Hoades looked up at his hands resting on top of his derby hat.

"Yes, of course. May I come in?"

John Little gestured the man toward the other chair in the room and the moment Hoades sat down, John Little performed a slight unsettling bow in front of him, his two pistols now crossed at his heart.

"I, sir, am John Little. I am at your disposal to dispose of whomever you wish." This line always caused him to smile at himself. "My fees are simple and fair. I take five hundred dollars a week working in town plus hotel and fare for myself and of course livery for my horse. If I got to chase some *sauvage* out into the wilderness there, then it goes up to six hundred. If there is a price on the man's head, and I chase him into the arms of the law, then you can keep the reward for yourself, for I will never be a lowly bounty hunter. However, I will ask you to sign a short contract drawn up by a reliable attorney, stating both your intentions and my own and relieving me of any legal responsibility for the outcome of our affairs together. Furthermore I will not kill women nor children nor Indians unless they shoot at me first. And if for some perverse reason you should choose not to pay my fee once my task has been completed to your satisfaction...but you look like an honorable man to me, Mr. Hoades, so why go into that bit of unpleasant business before we've even gotten started."

With this memorized speech John Little had begun all of his business that almost always ended in someone's death. He never did finish the last sentence, and it was meant for effect only, as he had never been cheated of his fee yet. After seeing the carnage he was capable of inflicting in a very short time usually the last thing anyone would think of was reneging on his fee.

Placing his pistols back in his shoulder holster he sat down in the armchair and leaned forward with a concerned look, couching his head in his hands and inching his face closer to Hoades own sweaty cheeks.

"Now what exactly can I do for you, Mr. Hoades?" He whispered. "I put myself at your service. Consider my pistols an extension of your own will, whatever that may be, and my own brain and eyes merely a tool of your determination and scope. We will be steady as we go here, I can assure you that, for I hate the sight of blood and the word massacre is not in my vocabulary. But tell me, what kind of killing can I do for you? Is it personal or is it business? Although I don't mind saying, I prefer a straight deal of commerce as compared to a personal *vendetta*." John Little pulled even closer to Hoades. "If, for example, your wife has taken a fancy to another man and you want him removed from this world, well I suggest you do it yourself, for I have no intention of involving myself in any *histoire de l'amour*."

Jonathan Hoades leaned back and cleared his throat loudly before speaking. "Well, of course I don't want you to go killing any women or children or even Indians for that matter. And my wife doesn't have any fancy man, for God's sake, she's a good church going lady...what kind of man do you think I am anyway?"

"Just a bit of pleasantry to lighten up the heavy atmosphere in this darkened room, sir." John Little smiled.

144

"Oh...oh. Well, I suppose one must have a sense of humor in your line of...work."

"Doesn't hurt."

"I'll get to the point Mr. Little. Someone is planning on delivering a..." He fumbled for words. "...A *shitload* of gold to my bank."

"Folks feeling generous these days?"

"Well, I received this damn letter about a month ago. There it was, staring me in the face. At first I thought it was somebody's idea of a joke, talking about an *exchange of honor between gentlemen* and other such nonsense and I didn't pay it no mind. But then one of their henchmen showed up in town and burst in my office and started waving his pistol around and saying I would be the first to go if I didn't go along with their plan. And a short time after that someone killed one of my mares — slit her throat right in my stable and left a note threatening my family. And well, I didn't want any more trouble so I agreed. Now I'm part of this crazy plan but I'm starting to thinking this might be too much for me to handle. It's all utterly insane and I figured you could help. After all, they've got their gunmen so why shouldn't I?"

"Never though of myself as a *gunman*, per se sir. Can't say that I really appreciate the term. But I am always sorry to hear when valuable horseflesh has been butchered for no apparent reason. Sure as hell wasn't that horses' fault."

"You see, Mr. Little..." Jonathan Hoades turned to peer behind him and then lowered his voice: "Normally I'd just have the sheriff put a few

145

deputies in the bank for a few weeks. But there's a...well, I guess I got to tell you. They say that if I go along that I can keep ten percent of the damn gold and that's a hefty chunk of change believe me. But I'm putting up a lot of cash myself in the bargain and if something goes wrong...I mean, one bank already failed in this town - The Commercial Bank of Guthrie - and I don't want to be the second. They're liable to lynch me if that happens."

John Little looked at his fingernails, rubbing them together fast, thinking about crickets. This was a different twist to his usual fare. Typically, he was called in after the fact, to capture or to eliminate rustlers or thieves, not to oversee some shady deal and make sure that it didn't lead to the ruin of an enterprise.

"If I understand you correctly, sir, you don't want me to kill anybody? You want me to prevent someone from killing you while you enrich your coffers? Is that it?"

"That's exactly it Mr. Little. If nothing happens I'll be completely satisfied."

"I might remind you that if you hire me - whatever does or does not happen - you will still be obligated to pay my fee."

"I understand that, sir."

John Little cocked his head quizzically and looked at Hoades: "But if nothing happens - how might you be able to judge when my work is in fact completed. Gets kind of dicey, eh? Your so-called partners might just wait for me to leave Guthrie before coming back to bother you - and I

146

can't hang around here forever. In fact, I prefer to spend as little time in Oklahoma as I possibly can."

"The territory doesn't please you, sir?"

"Its personal. Nothing at all to do with this land."

"Oh...well as I understand it, the gold is only going to rest with me for two weeks and then its going to be sent off to Fort Smith, with a fully armed cavalry convoy."

"And why don't the cavalry just sit on this gold all the time its here. Seems the logical thing to do."

"Because no one must know about this gold - where it came from. It has to be cleaned up first - made respectable, so to speak. And, they might not appreciate me taking my ten percent. Government might want all of it."

"*Mon Dieu*, what the hell are you talking about Mr. Hoades? Whose gold are you referring to anyway?"

The president got up out of his chair and again peered out the door of John Little's room. When he was convinced that no one was anywhere within hearing range, he returned to his seat."

"According to what I'm meant to believe, this gold is strictly a matter of unfinished business between one government and another. It represents a surrender of sorts."

"A surrender of who? The Indians ain't got any gold to speak of."

"Well, in fact they do. Them and the rebels, Its really a surrender of the rebels I'm talking about."

"What rebels is that?"

"The Confederacy...the south...those rebels! What other rebels are there?"

"I believe *monsieur* that those rebels already surrendered back in the Appomattox courthouse, Virginia, some years ago, if I'm not mistaken," he sniggered.

"Mr. Little this is a serious matter and I hesitate to take you into my confidence...but I will because I have no other choice. You see there was a second government of the south, a secret government that never capitulated and one that even Robert E. Lee himself didn't know about. On September 19, 1864, some months before the war ended there was a federal wagon train crossing the Indian Territory heading up towards the federal depot at Lawrence, Kansas that was captured by that injun Brigadier General Stand Watie and his Cherokee rebel army at the second battle of Cabin Creek, right here in Oklahoma. And in that wagon train was carrying gold worth over a million and a half dollars. When the war ended some months later, it just never turned up. Vanished into thin air!"

"Didn't know there were no Indians fighting for the rebels. Seems kind of odd, *n'est-ce-pas?*"

"Most of the Indians they shipped out here to Oklahoma, to the so-called *Indian Territories*, before the war, were from the south anyway. Hell, quite a few were even slave owners themselves. Anyway, this Indian General Watie was the last of the rebel leaders to surrender in 1865 – without the gold of course."

"So what happened to it?"

"Well that's just it, no one knew...until now that is. Some say that in the last days of 1865 they smuggled that gold down into Mexico with the idea of bribing the emperor Maximillian into coming in on the side of the Confederacy and opening a western assault against the Union with the Mexicans getting Texas back as part of the bargain But before a deal could be struck, Juarez and his boys made short shrift out of Emperor Maximillan - set him up against a wall and let them Mexican muskets do their work. And Juarez, him being called the Abe Lincoln of Mexico and all, he wanted nothing to do with damn slave owners and so they say his government just kept the gold and said nothing. But now it turns out it was all hidden right here in Oklahoma all these years and they want to strike a deal. And if I play the middleman I might just come out of this some kind of hero."

"And who is striking this deal? And why do it right here in Oklahoma?"

"Because Oklahoma is still Federal territory - no snooping state government to get involved. It was negotiated in Washington, I believe, or maybe New Orleans. He says that he's got a letter from the Secretary of Commerce no less authorizing me to give him a big chunk of real Federal currency and in return he's turning over the gold to shore up the government reserves. It's a clear and simple business deal - just like that. I mean, you can't have all that gold floating around or it's liable to upset the currency. See what I mean?"

149

"Not really Mr. Hoades and I don't suppose that matters much. But I would like to know to whom they're planning on doing this deal with? General Lee is long gone - Jeff Davis too, if I remember."

"Durand, General Durand."

John Little sat dumfounded on the chair next to his bed, his hands frozen in mid air, staring at the man. The banker looked uneasy.

"Durand?" He finally said. "Did you say Durand?"

"Why yes I did, sir, General Abel Durand."

"From..."

"...New Orleans. Do you know the man? Must be old as the hills by now."

John Little stood up and paced the room, his eyes wide as saucers, saying nothing.

"Can't say that I ever heard of the man either," said Hoades. "But I got a funny feeling about the whole thing, the way its been set up. This Durand insisted that there be no Federal troops here when he drops off the gold and makes the exchange. And I got a funny feeling about the whole damn deal."

"And why is that, sir? " asked John Little, finally able to speak. "If you do not know this man Durand as you say?"

"Because I fought at Gettysburg and don't trust any rebel worth a damn," said Hoades.

"So why not call the whole thing off and get the Federal Marshall down here instead of me."

"Because, it just might be for real." Hoades smiled widely. "And first and foremost, I am a businessman, sir."

When father Bachet married Rose O'Keefe and Abel Durand in a brief ceremony in the Vendee Catholic church, the bride had to be held up on each side by her fiancée and his man Carpis, and when it came time to say *I do* she merely opened her mouth and vomited, too drunk or ashamed to talk. Father Bachet was about to say something about the sanctity of the church when Durand handed him a one hundred dollar gold piece and told Carpis to stay behind and clean up his new wife's mess. Once the bride, groom and priest had walked out of the church, Carpis started scraping the vomit under a pew with his boot.

After that debauched ceremony, Durand, Carpis and Rose left Vendee the next morning in a covered carriage to move out to the former farm of John O'Keefe's which now belonged to Durand. Settled in at the farm were a few other ex-confederates - decommissioned prison guards of Andersonville - who had been bivouacked in the fields. Rose O'Keefe spent most of her time in a drunken daze.

In truth, Abel Durand did have one bar of Confederate gold but it was not the huge stash of gold that General Stand Waitie had taken at the second battle of Cabin Creek. No, Durand's gold bar was simply stolen from the officer's safe at Andersonville Prison the day before Federal troops arrived and liberated the hellhole. But when Carpis had come into Jonathan Hoades office shortly after slitting the throat of the man's horse and dumped that gold bar on his desk it made the whole story plausible and Hoades' greed overtook his fear.

Chapter 11

John Little awoke late, as was his custom, pleased to find himself resting on a comfortable horsehair mattress in a decent hotel bed. The bed was made of arched brass, the walls covered in a scarlet paper covering and John Little smiled and stretched his arms lazily. This was the one part of a work that involved endless amounts of traveling (and a fair share of it spent camping out over open ground in all kinds of unholy weather) that especially comforted him: staying in one of the few fine hotels that sparsely dotted the west wherever some boomtown entrepreneur had the audacious ambition to set up a really fine frontier establishment, embellishing it with steaming hot water for tub baths and even selling good cigars at the front desk. John Little was a man ready to take full advantage of whatever small luxuries came his way in this tragic world.

Reaching out from his brass bed, he unlatched and swung open the door to his room. The only noise coming from downstairs in the Hotel lobby was the loud ticking of an imposing grandfather clock. Listening to nearly a minute of ticking, he then yelled from his bed for the hotel boy who came scrambling up the stairs and stood just outside the door to the room, wearing an ill fitting and highly incongruous squire's uniform.

"Yes sir, Mr. Little. Something I can get for you?"

"Son, you can fetch me a pitcher of warm water for washing up and some hot coffee and eggs, *s'il vous plait*." Although thrown off by the

French for a moment, the boy quickly scampered away.

It was almost noon. With the hours he kept, John Little could never have been a successful rancher or farmer but few men dared mock him for his nocturnal ways or fancy dress. In Denver, where he lived with Qwing So, his was often the last candle seen burning late into the night while he read his poetry, made his killing plans, shined his boots and cleaned his guns. If he had a particularly long journey ahead of him that would oblige him to make an early morning start, more than likely he would mount his bay while still half asleep, just full of enough coffee to hold him upright. If his enemies, of which few were left alive, knew of his vulnerability at these early hours - eyes almost closed, nearly drifting off to sleep and often coming close to falling off his own horse – they could easily have ambushed him.

For most working men of the west, the early morning was the prime time for alertness and efficiency, unless they were nursing a hangover from a wicked nights' drunk, which John Little never was, not ever touching a drop of hard liquor. Getting an early start on the day was the very quality that sent men to test their mettle on the frontier to begin with. This habit of rising with the crack of dawn epitomized the frontier spirit - the drive and ambition to conquer a new day, a new piece of land or twenty more hard miles of a cattle drive. With saloons and whorehouses not opening until noon, there was no place else for a man to go in the morning except to work, be it branding cattle or mining silver or gold. And come sundown, when he might have built up a thirst for whiskey or women or more than likely both, the swinging doors of the saloons welcomed him.

In Denver, folks presumed John Little to be just another one of the many newly arrived easterners who had followed the silver rush. This was partially true, as he did arrive with Uncle George and his pack of whores some years back. In actual fact the strong inflection in John Little's voice was a combination of the thick Irish brogue picked up from his Uncle George, mixed in with the twirling tongue of his mother's Arcadian French. Still in the habit of peppering his speech with more than a few French words, he was inclined to evoke the name of the lord with *"Mon Dieu!"* when the world got the best of him, which it rarely did.

To all appearances, he was a dedicated family man even if he did have a Chinese wife who spoke English just like any real American, whatever that might be, and they lived quietly with their baby boy, Victor. Folks figured him to be some kind of stock trader or salesman, out of town for long stretches at a time and never once seen drunk in his Uncle George O'Keefe's saloon. There was even talk of his running for mayor, mainly because he looked the part: his slicked back blond hair starting to go silver at the temples and his fine fitting suits and high boots. Folks thought Denver could use a mayor who looked like that, maybe even run for Senator once statehood came, which it surely would.

John Little took the luxury of washing himself daily, something almost unheard of in the west, and he kept his hair smartly cut, dousing himself liberally with an imported toilet water that always spooked his

155

horse, a big bay appropriated down in Texas after he had killed its owner, a notorious horse thief. His moustache was short and trimmed and he was vain enough to stash away in his saddlebags a small pair of scissors and tin mirror so that even when camping out he could make himself more elegant than most paid killers, who generally took little interest in their appearance. Their looks were sometimes so repugnant that often their employers were prompted to pay their reckoning swiftly and be done with them. But this was not the style John Little had so carefully cultivated. His was the opposite: he was the dandy of gunfighters, owning three identical black pinstriped suits, replacing one if it became too tattered for his high sartorial standards. His Uncle George, a caricature of a jovial saloon keeper and whoremaster in his velvet suits and crimson vest if there ever was one, had instilled in him the need for a man to present a formidable picture to society and to other men, no matter what he intended on being. After all, hadn't he noticed early on that the most thieving politicians who came to visit Uncle George's bordello back on Canal Street were undoubtedly the best dressed? And most importantly, he had promised himself that when the day came for killing Durand, he would not be dressed like any *pig farmer*.

In this way he had set himself apart and, in his opinion, above others he hunted in his deadly trade; most of whom lived on the range and whose wardrobe consisted of whatever they were wearing on their back, whose filthy long-johns might leave their skin some half dozen times a year if they got near a tub of warm enough water, although many

156

desperadoes chose to bathe with their underwear on and a gun within short reach.

To mistake John Little for a gambler, was the most deadly error any man could make, although understandable enough given his wide brimmed black beaver hat and glinting mother-of-pearl cufflinks. John Little detested professional gamblers with a passion and could be unreasonably vicious with them if they crossed his path. One evening in east Texas he had nearly wiped out a whole table of poker players when in fact only one man had foolishly drawn a pistol when John Little had refused to pay up at the end of the game, casually calling the man (and his presumed partners) "*sale tricheurs* lower than serpents." A fourth man had been left cowering in the corner, pleading for his life, explaining that he had only just sat down at the game like John Little himself. Finally, when his rage passed, he put away his Remingtons and walked out of the saloon, taking no heed of the two dead men left on the table whose hands still gripped their holstered pistol butts. Their blood was quickly turning the green felt a murky brown and a third man, still clutching his hidden pistol, moaned on the floor beneath the table with a stomach wound that would kill him in a long, painful time.

The career of a *gunfighter*, a man who knows how to skillfully shoot another man dead and will do so for hire, for cash - who can guiltlessly walk out of a bar, away from a dying men's blood and moans, required a cold bloodedness not generally found in most men, no matter how tough they might consider themselves. Many would be killers were themselves just bitter ex-Civil War soldiers roaming the west, fresh from the killing fields of Virginia, who might manage to kill one or two men before being shot dead themselves, their anger often making them careless. Or a hired killer might just be another victim of the unforgiving frontier ways, that in one harsh winter could destroy a man's hopes and dreams when a whole family was wiped out by disease or hostile Indians, and such bereavement might set him on a mortal trail of blood letting, caring little for his own or anyone else's life.

Indian haters, in fact, were especially numerous among professional killers, particularly among the Texans. Any man can be pushed to kill once, over a card game or stolen horse or a woman, but to accept without question that each step away from the carnage he has just caused only takes him back on the trail to the next job, the next round of bullets to be aimed at a soon to be shattered man's body, now that required the exact *sang froid* with which John Little was both blessed and cursed.

The unique and deadly services of these men, these killers, were valued higher than almost any other trade on the frontier with the exception of those few stock men who had the innate ability to recognize a sound horse from one likely to go lame in the middle of *nowhere* (which was nearly anywhere between St. Louis and San Francisco) by the smell in a horses nostrils, or the way a horse stood while drinking water from the trough. Next to that kind of horse sense, a gunman's talents were valued above all other occupations. A gunman was a detective, an insurance company agent and even the law itself in many parts of the west. And as ironic as it may seem, it was the gunman's ability to carry out a contract to completion until another man lay dying that finally led the way towards more lawful institutions tightening their grip on the wide-open towns west of the Mississippi. And like the blindfolded figure of lady justice herself, a paid gunman or *regularizer* was blind to everything except the stack of bills he was handed at the end of the day after the killing was all done. A tradition upheld by highly paid attorneys for generations to come who succeeded in stealing the land and everything underneath it from its original inhabitants.

In a territory as vast as the western frontier, running from the Mexican border along Texas and Arizona up to the Lakota Sioux dominated Dakotas, and over to Oregon's vast forests, a gunman's fame could still spread as fast as the telegraph allowed. The media of the day had already begun to immortalize the names of a handful of these men whose notoriety had been set aflame back east by the sparks of fallacious dime novels packed with erroneous myths that grew wild on the frontier. Beginning with rebel guerilla misfits who had been left on the losing side of the civil war such as Frank and Jesse James and the psychotic Texan John Wesley Harding, western gunmen lore soon included the Brooklyn born teenage assassin, Billy the Kid, the gambling Indian fighter Wild Bill Hickok and a host of lesser known personages with equally fanciful names. And there were the gangs as well: the Daltons, the Youngers, Butch Cassidy and the Hole in the Wall Gang; not to mention those equally vicious gunmen who managed to do their killing in the name of the law like the Earp brothers and bowler hatted Bat Masterson, who incongruously ended his days writing a sports column for a New York journal.

But John Little was something different, something modern, neither lawman nor criminal. He worked for stockman's associations losing cattle to rustlers or some boomtown's defense committee set on cleaning out its undesirables or, as now in Guthrie, Oklahoma, to protect a burgeoning frontier bank about to receive a large shipment of gold bullion. And as with most of his ilk, there was little known about who the man called John Little really was except that you could contact him by telegram care of a whorehouse in Denver, fancifully named *O'Keefe's Emporium II,* and that if your telegram arrived on a Monday, chances were that by the middle of the next week, John Little himself would be strolling into your office with saddle bags over his shoulder and two Remington 44's across his chest, hidden under a long tan duster to protect his fine clothes.

John Little's credentials lay in his reputation as a cold-blooded killer for hire, his references irrefutable from the fact that he had lived long enough to gain such fame. After all, any cowboy could kill a man, getting the drop on him in a drunken saloon shoot out. But to kill enough men so that your name started getting attached to the very act of gun fighting itself, well, that was the beginning of a goddamn bonafied career and the kind of work that John Little was hired to do suited few other men so well: he being the first of the corporate killers, so to speak.

Chapter 12

Durand rode into Guthrie accompanied by one other of his ragtag soldiers who held aloft a ratty white flag and it was not Carpis. John Little watched the scene from the roof of the feed store across from the bank. When Durand got directly in front of the bank, the soldier at his side started playing the bugle in his hand, although he seemed to have no proficiency on the instrument; he just kept toot, tooting until Jonathan Hoades finally emerged from the bank.

"Sir, I come in here on a white flag of truce which I hope you will honor," said Durand still mounted on his horse.

"And sir, I might remind you that there is no war in this territory as far as I know of so I don't quite understand what this here truce is all about," said Hoades looking around him nervously. "And where is the gold?" He asked.

"I have never surrendered," said Durand. "And I never will. But I intend to leave with that U.S. currency that I was promised."

"But where is the Gold?" demanded Hoades. "This was to be an exchange. You think I'm some kind of damn fool?"

"Sir, I have more important business then to discuss the details of this transaction with you and I advise you to give me that federal currency unmolested and so we might go on your way. "

"You listen to me now," said Hoades. "This is the Territory of Oklahoma, part of the United States of America and that currency which is safely locked in my vaults will remain there until you produce the gold bullion as promised.

Durand slowly dismounted and pulled the Winchester rifle out from the scabbard hanging from his saddle before walking the few steps to stand directly in front of Hoades. "Sir, may I direct your attention to the far end of town, to the hill that rises just there."

Hoades looked over yonder but saw nothing unusual.

Durand smiled. "Fear not, for I do not fire this rifle in attack," quickly firing three times in the air. Within minutes a flatbed wagon drawn by six horses and two drivers and mounted with a Gattling gun roared into town and braked to a stop right in front of the bank. Squatting next to the shiny mounted gun and holding on to the trigger was Carpis. The wagon pulled right up next to where Durand was standing. And the gun was pointed directly at Hoades.

"Sir, I have finished my negotiations and now I will hand the matter over to my troops to handle. I wish you God's mercy and wash my hands of the matter." Durand turned and mounted and rode just behind the wagon. The drivers of the wagon, the bugler, and even Carps looked slightly confused as to what to do next. John Little stayed put, lying on the roof with the Sharps Buffalo rifle mounted on a small turret in front of him. He had not expected Durand to leave so suddenly and now the two drivers blocked any clear shot of Carpis. He only hoped Jonathan Hoades would hold his ground.

Carpis finally spoke. "Well, you all heard what General Durand said so let's get going."

"Get going where?" said Hoades.

"I mean…let's get going with the money. Durand said you be full of cash in there and we aim to take it with us, isn't that right boys." The three others remained silent.

"I am giving you one warning and that is all," said Hoades. "You are surrounded and no one is going to allow you to rob this bank today. There are armed guards both inside and outside the bank who will not allow you to escape. Your plan, if you have any goddamn plan, is pure lunacy. Get the hell out of here while you still can."

Carpis jumped off the wagon and pinned Hoades arm behind him. Hoades grimaced but more from the terrible stench of the man than from the pain from his twisted arm. "Now I'm gonna go in there and see if there's any cash in there that belongs to General Durand. And if anyone bothers me, my friends here are gonna start shooting this damn Gattling gun right at you and blow you to little pieces." One of the drivers took a seat next to the gun. "Hey bugler sound your horn," said Carpis. "Cause we be attacking just like in the battle." Carpis smiled at himself. Having the bugler sound had been his own idea and he was sure that Durand would like it. The bugler brought the horn to his lips and started his pitiful toot-toot, when two shots came from across the street. For a moment everything was quiet.

"Hey bugle boy, I told you to sound the charge. Ain't no little rifle shot gonna scare us," said Carpis. "We be soldiers, ain't we?"

But when the bugle failed to sound, Carpis let go of Hoades arm and walked over to nudge the mounted man's leg at which the bugler fell off his horse and Carpis saw that half his head was shot off. Hoades scampered inside the bank as another shot took one of the drivers off the wagon. Carpis surveyed the dead man and saw he had been shot clearly through the eyes.

"Holy Jeez..." he yelled as he jumped beneath the wagon for cover but at that moment the driver that was left alive whipped his horses into action and the wagon was speeding out of town leaving Carpis cowering on the street with his head in his arms. John Little waited until the wagon was too far for Carpis to regain his position next to the Gattling gun and then shot the man off the wagon as the team of horses galloped on.

Carpis crawled frantically behind the water trough in front of the bank and began firing wildly with his six-shooter while trying to load the shotgun held in his other hand with a cartridge clamped in his teeth.

John Little had exited the roof and circled the town, entering the bank from the back with a prearranged signal with Hoades opening the door for him.

"We got the one you shot off the wagon. Badly wounded but I suppose we'll still be able to hang him. Don't you think there's more of them?" asked Hoades. "They couldn't have expected to rob us with just four men now could they?"

"I supposed they thought that Gattling gun would scare the bejesus out of you," said John Little. "Wonder if the damn thing even worked."

"But what if it had worked?" said Hoades. "And here you sent all those armed guards away."

"I prefer to work alone," said John Little.

"You call this work?" said Hoades.

"Up till this moment," said John Little. "But now its personal."

John Little left the bank and again circled the town and came out on the other side of the street with both Carpis and the bank in front of him. Carpis' shotgun had misfired - cartridges gone damp from too much riding in the rain - but John Little heard the two clicks of his hammers as loud as an earthquake. He walked calmly over to where the sound came from, in front of the bank by the water trough. Carpis was lying flattened on the ground on the other side, hiding his bulk as best he could. When he saw John Little's face looming down on him from above the rusty water he could do nothing but smile.

"Bad powder. Imagine it musta gone damp what with all this rain we've been having."

"Imagine so," said John Little "Terrible weather, no?"

"But you wouldn't shoot a man lying defenseless on the ground, would you, mister?"

"I reckon some might say that weren't fair play," said John Little. "That a man wasn't given a sporting chance - like even the worst of men deserved some kind of...consideration. What you got to say about that? You think there's some truth there?"

John Little was pointing the two barrels of his Remingtons directly at

Carpis' nose. He held the guns steadily with his gloved hands and his expression had every similarity to that of a cat playing with a mouse, minutes before gulping down the thing whole.

"I suspect that's what they might say," said Carpis, still smiling, his own mouth long broken clean of any whole teeth. "And I suppose it ain't the best thing for a man's reputation, I suppose? Killing another man without giving him some kind of a real chance to defend his self, I mean."

"I suppose not. So let's just say...another day, eh?"

When John Little stepped aside the glaring noonday sun suddenly blinded Carpis and when he raised his hand to shield his burning eyes, why... John Little was completely gone, out of sight. Carpis squinted hard again trying to keep out the harsh light, rubbing his eyes ferociously but still seeing no one standing over him. John Little and the Remington s that had just been pointing down at him had disappeared. As quickly as he could, considering his bulk, Carpis reached into the ammo pocket of his vest and pulled out two fresh shotgun cartridges, smelling them first for dampness and then, still hugging the side of the water trough with his back, as quietly as possible cracking open his shotgun, expelling the ruined cartridges and reloading the two fresh ones. He stood up slowly, eyes peering over the water trough, looking down toward the end of the dusty main street of the town where the heat rippled off chips of mica and sand in an undulating mirage.

Then he was sure he saw John Little walking fast, down a ways, crossing the street, his back to him now and still carrying his big guns in front of him. Carpis grunted and rose to his feet, the long shotgun in front of him, crouching as he slid past the wooden railings where horses were tied, stamping their feet in the heat, and flicking flies with their tails. The safety of the water trough was fifteen feet behind him when he realized that the hazy image he was following, supposing it to be John Little, was just a young boy, tall for his age and wearing a big hat, lugging groceries to his ma across the street. And then, he heard John Little's voice behind him, calling out his name. He swung around his head, nearly wrenching his neck to see John Little lying on the other side of the water trough, his two Remingtons held in both hands and pointed in front of him, steadied by his elbows resting in the dirt.

"*Mon Dieu*, another day sure comes quickly around here," said John Little.

Carpis pulled the shotgun up and around but before he could get it pointed down in front of him, John Little shot him in each knee and Carpis collapsed as if all the air were let out of him, his own shotgun going off double-barreled into the air as it hit the ground and blowing off most of his nose.

John Little was astride him now, his knee on Carpis' chest. Calmly he put one Remington away and pulled out his father's Derringer from his vest pocket shoving the barrel into the hold that was once Carpis' nose.

"Seems you lost your nose," he said calmly. "No matter, I doubt you ever cleaned it anyway."

Carpis gurgled some response and tried to lift his arm and John Little

167

shot him through the wrist with his Remington.

"I wanted to tell you a goodnight story," said John Little. "About a man named John O'Keefe and how you shot him like a coward…but you smell too bad to waste any more time with."

Carpis' eyes widened and than John Little pulled the small trigger of the derringer and the bullet went clear through his brain and into the street. He stood and examined his own soiled suit; maybe he'd get it brushed and cleaned back in Denver, or throw this one away and send for a new one from San Francisco.

Jonathan A. Hoades had arranged something of a send-off for John Little, both to thank him for his most excellent and efficient work and to introduce him to the rest of his cigar-smoking friends, who might one day benefit from his deadly labors. The event was held in the Guthrie Hunting Lodge, located on a butte at the far side of town. The room was wood paneled and opulent, the walls covered with the heads of deer and elk and a vast assortment of hunting rifles lining the walls. A fine dinner was served, on real china with silver cutlery and John Little liked that, but when the men started talking politics, it hindered his digestion. They were fearful of the effect the newly arrived immigrant population would have on the territory, the frenzied rush for claims on land they presumed should be in their own domain. Finally, Hoades himself got up to speak in front of the group. Standing to face the twenty odd men sitting around the long table, he began to read a prepared speech, thanking John Little for his services and then, at the close of it, handing him a small velvet sac full of gold coins. John Little took the bag in hand and surveyed the well-heeled group before him. They so resembled the same kind of men who used to come in through the back door at his Uncle's bordello in New York and then were ready to run him out of town when the political winds shifted. For a moment he was speechless. Although this was a hunter's club he was the surely the most skillful hunter among them: an expert when it came to the killing of men. He looked over the heads of the well heeled assemblage and cleared his throat loudly before beginning to recite in a booming voice, startling the men and causing a few to choke on their cigars.

"The great master and cosmos are well as they go! The heroes and good-doers are well! The known leaders and inventors and the rich owners and pious and distinguished may be well..."

These men, although rich and use to the fineries of life - or at least whatever fineries might be available in Guthrie - would hardly be considered cultured according to anybody's standards and read little but figures on the bills for cattle sales. Not a one among them had ever read any poetry he could remember - nor would he admit it if he had - and no one of this group of Guthrie's gentility could recognize the words of Walt Whitman if their life depended on it. These frontier burghers smiled nervously at one another, not understanding how a man who just killed several men, who would just as soon empty his revolvers into someone else's chest as into a stump of wood, who collected his gold for such work guiltlessly and with a smile, would be saying these kind of fancy words to them. They had hoped the evening might turn into a debauch, with whisky and fine cigars and some of the whoring girls brought down from the local saloon. Beaver hunting, they called nights like this.

But John Little went on: "The known leaders and inventors and the rich owners and pious and distinguished may be well..."

Some of these men now thought he might be complementing them on their high standing and fortunes, and they harrumphed and *here-here'd* one another with boisterous pats on the back.

"But..." John Little raised his voice and his eyes widened. "There is more account than that...there is strict account of all!"

The local stockman who set the pitiful prices for the sheep and cattle brought to market by the small ranchers and herders leaned close to Jonathan Hoades, sitting next to him.

"I think he wants more money, Hoades. What do you think?"

"I don't know what the hell he wants. Maybe he just wants to speak," said Hoades. It takes a strange sort of man to do that sort of work. Probably got some kind of dementia."

"I suppose," said the other man. "We'd better let him go on, get whatever he has to say off his chest."

By now John Little was reading from a book and standing on a chair. "The living look upon the corpse with their eyesight, but without eyesight lingers a different living and looks erroneously on the corpse." He paused and then closed the small book of verse in front of him, stepped down off the chair and strolled out of the Hunting Lodge.

"You be sure to come back for the hanging," yelled Jonathan Hoades after him. "When we catch that old rebel Durand."

Chapter 13

John Little knew where to find Judge Durand, lying wounded back in Vendee. His only fear was that he'd up and die on him before he finally caught up to him; his first shot having caught him square in the shoulder. The judge, lay in his bed coughing up huge clumps of death into the spittoon at his side. The new parish priest had already been sent for to give him last rights, but it would not be Father Bachet who had been reassigned to the Arizona territory, converting Indians under the blistering sun and having a hard time convincing the Yuma tribe that hell could be any hotter than the desert they called home sweet home. Somehow or another news of his and Durand's doings had reached members of the archdiocese back in St. Louis who were not pleased that a man of their own cloth was filling his own coffers and not theirs.

When the priest called on Judge Durand, the Mexican servant girl crossed herself and let him in, pointing to the Judge's room and following softly some steps behind.

"You will not be needed here, senorita. I have come to take the Judge's confession for he is not far from meeting our Lord."

"Si, padre." She bowed and left.

He could hear the wheezing sound of Durand's breathing before he even entered the room and pulled up a chair next to the pale figure on the bed and sat down. The old man's eyes opened up, strangely youthful and searching, waiting for a new world somewhere.

"Are you the priest? The new one?"

John Little took off the priest's collar he had borrowed from the church and bent close to the judge's ear: "You can call me Petit Jean O'Keefe for I am the son of John O'Keefe, the man you had murdered right in front of me, his only son. The man whose body you spit on as he lay dying; the man whose grieving widow you took as your own and whose daughter you ruined with the help of that wretched priest who drove her to madness and me, his son, sent away to a life of running whores and killing men for money. You're a rotten son of a bitch and I'm here to kill you good for once and for all. I'm no angel of mercy."

The old man's eyes widened but he said nothing.

John Little had said this same speech to himself countless number of times and the words raced out of him in a torrent of hatred: "You who have had it all, born to wealth and privilege, but still evil and dispensing misery and being a true judge of no man, with no sense of justice and an aversion to mercy. You've turned all that you've touched into something hateful, so now I'm here to blow you away to kingdom come, so help me God."

"Go ahead, you little bastard," wheezed the old man. "I'll see you rot in hell with me. My man Carpis will follow you down and avenge me, of that I'm sure. You will never have another night's peaceful sleep, sir."

"Ah, but that's not so certain," said John Little smiling. "Your man Carpis, your mangy dog, is dead and buried back in Guthrie, it seems he lost his nose and took a bullet through his puny brain before he could even raise his shotgun. Suppose you didn't get to see none of that as you scampered out of town with a bullet in you once the shooting started. But he left a going away present for you." Petit Jean took the bloody cloth from his vest pocket and opened it. The shriveled and filthy finger fell on the judge's chest, who gasped with fright. "I suppose this was the same trigger finger he used to kill my pa."

John took the derringer from the inside pocket of his priest's black funeral suit. "This was my father's gun - a present from his own Union regiment and now I aim to stick it by your ear and pull the trigger. The last sound you will hear, you rebel bastard, will be the slamming of your brains into your fine wallpaper."

But the old man was feistier than Petit Jean imagined and under the covers he swung up a pearl-handled Colt 45. Quickly, he managed to shoot off one chamber but it blew off into the ceiling, missing John Little but setting the bed linen on fire. The flakes from the ruined ceiling plaster rained onto the old man's face as John Little pulled the burning covers off him and easily wrestled the pistol away. Durand was naked on the bed now but there was no manliness about him, his skin hairless and splotched and between his legs was the penis of a baby, almost non-existent.

The old man scrambled to cover himself.

"Is that what's been brewing that hatred inside of you all these years? You've got the pecker of a bird there."

"You can't kill me! I'm your mother's husband. I'm your legal

174

stepfather, you bastard! I'm a judge from the state of Louisiana..."

John Little stood there thinking about his own life while the Judge continued to rave on, thinking about his father and the night Durand had missed him by a mile only to be shot dead by Carpis moments later. He was thinking about his mother and her wet brain and his sister Antoinette, who was God knows where now. About Uncle George and his thirteen whores and Qwing So who was waiting for him back in Colorado.

"Finally, you're too pitiful to kill," he said to Durand and he got up and started walking toward the bedroom door. "I think I've wasted my life thinking of this moment. It was so real I could almost taste it. And now..."

But then in an instant, it all came back to him so excruciatingly painful he couldn't bear it: John O'Keefe down on his knees, holding his bloody chest while Durand lectured him on the need for justice and spitting down on him and then the terrible sound of his father's last gasp. And that day in the hearing with Marshall Barkin when Durand had dropped the gold pieces at his mother's feet and how he had scrambled to gather the rolling coins and hand them to his mother, thinking it would make some difference in their lives. But none of it made any difference now, for his family had been ruined forever and finally.

John Little swung around quickly and in three long steps placed the derringer smack next to the old man's head, pulled the trigger and blew the Judge's bloody brains into the snowy depths of the soft feather pillow.

He stood there at Durand's side for a long time, waiting for someone to come, to notice, to smell the gunpowder with him, to witness Durand's pale corpse and to celebrate with him. When the door creaked open, he swung around fast pointing the derringer in front of him, one bullet still left. In the twilight he could make out a figure standing in back of the door. It was a teenage boy in a nightdress whose whole body was trembling as he stared at the bed. John Little stood there looking at the boy, not saying anything and then, behind the boy, his own mother appeared, haggard and gray haired, with not a speck off beauty left that drink hadn't picked off her face.

"You best get back to bed, Robert," she said and the boy ran off. She walked past John Little and over to Durand and laid her hand on his bloody head. She wobbled on her feet, plainly drunk.

"He wasn't such a bad husband," she slurred.

"Ma, I promised..."

"You finally done it, *Mon Dieu*," she said. "I always knew you would. I knew you had that derringer from the first night."

John Little said nothing more.

"Give me the gun," she said. "I'll say it was me."

He dropped the gun on the bed. "Don't do that ma," he said. "They'll hang you."

"I doubt it," she said. "You better be getting out of Vendee and staying out. There's death around you, my son, and I suspect there always will be."

"But how...how could you do it? How could you be with him after

176

Pa? I don't know…it set my world upside down."

"Son, I lost everything good and pure in my life so I could only embrace evil. It was the only power that could damn me totally and erase all I lost. Evil was stronger than my grief."

"I don't understand."

"I think you do, better then you know. You better go now. I am no longer worthy to be your mother and you are not worthy to be my son. We are both damned but follow me and I'll lead you to safety."

The bells of the small chapel were ringing and the streets were mostly deserted. It was early Sunday morning and the cowboys were still *siested* from their Saturday night drunk. Petit Jean walked down the dusty road with his mother.

"Come with me Ma," he said. "Come with me to Denver and meet my wife and behold your grandchild. Leave this damn place forever."

"They say your Uncle George runs whores up there," said his ma. "I hope you aren't involved in that sinful traffic."

"Ma, I just killed your husband in cold blood and you're worried that I'm running whores, *Mon Dieu.*"

"A sin is a sin."

"Not in this world, it isn't"

"I'm thirsty," she said. "Reckon I'll get back to the house and have a drink."

"And what about Antoinette? Come with me and find her and make her well again. Make all of us well again."

177

"You may find Antoinette, Petit Jean, but you'll never see your sister again, son."

"I don't know, ma…"

John Little kissed his mother on both cheeks and left her at the door of the church although she gave no sign of entering. He turned around and walked towards the stable where his horse was waiting and rode out of town with his head down, not wanting to see the dusty streets of Vendee again if he could help it.

Rose O'Keefe went back to the house where Durand lay dead and picked up the Derringer Petit Jean had left on the bed. She laid her head on her second husband's corpse and considered getting her bottle and having a drink and than whispered *"Pardonez moi Mon Dieu"* as she put the Derringer in her mouth and fired off the second load without thinking anymore about anything.

As the century closed the lawlessness on the frontier was rapidly diminishing, but John Little was satisfied that with the vacuum of authority in most parts west of the Mississippi, he would continue to offer his services and increase his wealth; being able to leave his peaceful home and family every few months, reap death and destruction on whatever malcontents his gun hand might fall on and than return home. Ironically, he was convinced that this seasonable purging of the great violence within his soul had made him a stable father and gentle husband.

He was sure he knew enough of the law to avoid winding up with a rope around his own neck. Any bank, stockman's association or individual who employed his services, first had to sign a simple legal document attesting to the fact that they believed themselves or their property to be in mortal danger from such and such known desperado and that they hereby hired John Little to protect their rights as guaranteed under the Constitution of the United States. It was crime and punishment - pure and simple - owing more to the old testament of the Bible than to any precedent set by the Supreme Court of The United States. How could the law try to prevent robbery or murder by those who had no motivation by way of church or family not to commit heinous crimes? Most of the bad actors John Little eliminated had but a feeble sense of meaning to their flighty existence anyway, theirs being truly desperate lives: on the run under a handful of aliases, what few high times they had were to be found in smoky saloons with unwashed whores. It was folly for good citizens of the territory to think that putting the fear of punishment into a man's heart would bring law and order, when his chance of being apprehended for the most heinous crimes imaginable depended upon how fast his horse could carry him to a more lenient sheriff's jurisdiction. Frank and Jesse James had robbed trains and banks for nearly twenty years and that was in Missouri, a full-fledged State of the Union with an organized constable and judiciary. If it was not for the presence of the informer and assassin Bob Ford in their gang's midst, who knows - they might have gone on for another ten years or more likely even entered politics.

Still, common wisdom held that a grisly public execution served to dissuade a few of the more faint hearted would-be murderers who might be watching in the crowd but even that was uncertain considering the all consuming passion of the moment that prompted guns to start blazing. And a last-chance absolution of the soul was available to almost any man, guilty or innocent, who found himself standing on a loose plank of pinewood with a rope around his neck and a crowd waiting to hear the chilling crack of his vertebrae as he fell into the void, begging for his maker's forgiveness. What went through a man's mind before he took that drop into the infinite often brought out a touching eloquence when a doomed man humbly accepted all the hard luck that fate might have brought his way, still hoping that God in his mercy could see fit to let him through the gates of paradise even if his behavior here on earth had been less than, say, exemplary. Most hangmen had enough sense of drama to allow a condemned man to finish a memorable last phrase before springing the trap door beneath him and sending the poor bastard swinging and twitching his way into the hereafter.

Marshall Dan Barkin rode slowly into the town of Guthrie early morning, puzzled at the gathering crowd until he made out the newly erected pine scaffolding. Barkin was returning after an unsuccessful pursuit of the Dalton-Doolin gang who had been terrorizing the territory for years, finally losing them in the shrinking Indian Territory. Barkin was relieved this public hanging wasn't his doing, never having enjoyed having to stand up there on the scaffold in his now official capacity as U.S. Marshall. He parked his horse and stood with the others who stared up to the condemned man, his hands and legs tightly bound and the hangman standing next to him nonchalantly counting the knots on his noose. At least this was a more civilized hanging than others the sheriff had come across, where a sturdy oak and a cowboy's rope might be all there was to send a man into perdition - slowly.

The doomed man was sending his last thoughts out to the captive audience. He was an elegant speaker for an outlaw, but even so the crowd was growing restless, eager to get back to their morning chores. Standing to the side of the crowd, the Marshall noticed a particularly well-dressed man in a black suit and clean white shirt - a rare sight in these parts - with two gleaming Remington 44's visible inside his coat. Mistaking such a heavily armed man to be the sheriff of the town, Dan Barkin strolled over to exchange greetings and talk shop.

"What's this hombre up there done?" He asked

"Tried to rob a bank," said John Little. "I shot him off the wagon he was trying to escape in but than tried to steal a horse and get out of town – it seems folks don't care much about robbing banks but they sure don't like horse thieves around here. Judge sentenced him to hang for that alone."

"Jeez, they're still hanging them for stealing horses around here? Seems kind of harsh to me. Nowadays in most of the territory they throw their butt in the penitentiary in Kansas or at worse brand them on their backsides."

"Guess they're old fashioned in this town," said John Little.

"You the sheriff here then?"

"*Pas moi*. I just helped spoil the bank robbery."

"Bounty hunter then?"

"Not me...sort of regularizer."

"What's that supposed to mean?

John Little turned to face the old sheriff. "It means that I don't break no laws and a lot of men seem to end up dead or hung and the situation becomes, well, regular again."

"You get paid for this?"

"It isn't a sport." John Little smiled.

Barkin looked the man over and thought there was something oddly familiar about him.

"What be your name then Mister? In case I ever need some of this here...regularizing."

"John Little. You can wire me in Denver care of *O'Keefe's Emporium*, and Hoades, the bank president, can vouch for me. He seemed pretty satisfied with my work, I must say."

"Little? Yes, I believe I have heard of you already. Seems, you got quite a reputation. Folks say you never like to get the blood on your fine suit and you always wear a duster when you're working with a shotgun."

"I say why spoil a fine garment with some hombre's splattered insides?" John Little turned to face the formidable presence of Dan Barkin. The sheriff was getting on in years but Little could still sense plenty of power and determination in him and knew he was a man to be

182

reckoned with. He smiled. "Rest assured, you got no problem with me, Marshall. I don't hire myself out to take revenge on another man's wounded pride and I don't kill Indians neither. I figure I enforce the law - just like you - I'm just an extension of your own presence in these unlawful parts."

"Like hell you are. Where were you when I was hunting down the Doolin gang and killing off the Daltons. I didn't see you at Coffeyville when the bullets were pissing like rain."

"Can't say that I've had the pleasure of visiting the town. What happened there?"

"You been on the moon or what? You seen Bill Doolin in these parts?""

"Can you describe the man?"

"Black slouch hat, closely buttoned coats. Sometimes sports a waxed moustache."

"Can't say that I have. You see Marshall, that's a perfect example: you just don't have the time to do what I do. I might spend a week surveying a gambling saloon if there's a ripe rumor that some desperado is intent on coming to town and shooting the place to kingdom come on account of a lost game of cards. I doubt if you got that kind of time."

"Maybe if I was being paid your kind of money I could find that kind of time."

"Then maybe we will meet again," said John Little.

"It's a big territory."

"Been here a long time, Marshall?"

"Use to cover the whole territory from the Arkansas line down to the sooners living in Old Oklahoma. Had to throw them all out when the federal government opened up the land for settling. Most of them came right back on to their old farms come the land rush."

"Ever hear of a god forsaken place called Vendee?"

"Vendee...? Yeah, reckon I do; windswept place just over the Arkansas line. Never could figure out what state it really was in. In fact, if my memory still serves me, I've been there two times: first was some years ago when a young sodbuster got himself kilt during a card game by some New Orleans dandy, and the only reason I remember that is because just recently someone laid that same rebel in his grave. Why do you ask about Vendee?"

"Oh I don't know," said John Little. "Knew someone who lived there once, told me to stop by and visit if I was ever passing by. Doubt if I will though." He hesitated. "Marshall, you suppose you'll find the man that did it?"

"Did what?"

"Put that old rebel in his grave?"

"Not yet. They say he had a hired man used to do his dirty work for him, going by the name of Carpis, and no one seen him around either. Say the fellow stunk like hog piss. Some figure it was him who blew him away. Whoever did it killed his wife too while he was at it."

John Little blanched and steadied himself from falling down.

184

"What are you talking about, Marshall?" he asked dumbfounded.

"Found his wife's body next to his. Coulda been a suicide, coulda been murder, not really sure yet."

John Little began to feel his knees buckle under him as he pulled a handkerchief to wipe the cold sweat off his brow.

"*Au revoir*, Marshall, I best be moving." He said somberly.

"What the hell is that? Indian talk?"

"French," said John Little. "Learned it from my mother some years ago."

When Dan Barkin spotted John Little again in Denver some months after the hanging in Oklahoma, he was sure this was his man. The uncertainty which had haunted him for months had solidified somewhere on the road to Wichita when he had stopped his perplexed horse in the middle of a field of barley and proclaimed to no one but himself:

"Guldarn it! That was him - it was the boy all grown up into a killer. Was him who plugged his ma and that ol' bastard Durand."

Barkin was not one to harp on a man's reasons for killing but still he was needled by the death of Rose Durand. Why had John Little killed her as well? Of course, he could understand the murder of Judge Durand; in fact, if it had only been the judge he might have let it go himself or at least stuck the warrant under a sheath of federal papers as tall as the Smoky Mountains. Didn't the old man have it coming after all? He had killed the boy's father, had probably lied at that hearing so many years ago, had driven off the boy's sister to a life of whoring and insanity, and had

185

married his mother and then locked her in a house with her bottles and her shame.

Barkin stationed himself outside *O'KEEFE'S EMPORIUM* around dusk on a Sunday night. It seemed John Little had a habit of going in there and conferring with the owner of the place around dusk each evening. When Little walked out of the place Barkin cold cocked him on the side of the head and stopped his fall by placing his two arms under his shoulders and dragging him to a waiting horse. It was not the first time that Barkin had apprehended a criminal in such a manner and he was easily able to drape John Little's unconscious body across the saddle and silently walk the two horses out of town.

An hour later when John Little came to he was sitting with his back resting against a tree and his hands cuffed together in front of him. There was a small campfire going and a pot of coffee boiling on top of it. Dan Barkin sat staring at him, smiling.

"Hope I didn't give you too bad a goose egg back there..."

With his two hands bound together John Little felt the bump behind his right ear and noticed the caked blood coming off onto his fingers.

"But the last time I tried to arrest a man in his hometown, his friends got so aroused that they almost lynched me instead. So now, I prefer not to take any chances and just get out of town as quickly as possible."

"You got no business arresting me Marshall, I've broken no law of this territory or any other."

"Comes as a surprise to me, son. 'Cause last I hear killing your stepfather and mother breaks quite a few of them in my book."

"I never kilt my mother. She done it herself, she was not of this world anymore. And Judge Durand was no father to me - step or otherwise - not to mention the fact he was armed himself. I suppose no one noticed that revolver resting beneath his covers. Mon Dieu, nearly blew my own head off."

"We got a witness to the murder."

"And who might that be? God himself?"

"In fact it is the man's son - Robert E. Durand."

The hearing in Vendee was crowded and John Little said nothing in his defense. The only witness called was young Robert E. Durand, barely more then a boy but tall and thin like his father.

"He killed my daddy in cold blood, like a thief in the night. He gave my daddy less chance than they gives a steer in a slaughtering pen."

"And did you see him murder your stepmother as well?" Asked Marshall Barkin.

"Can't say that I did. He must have come back and finished the job later that night."

The Marshall was dumfounded and didn't know what to say. John Little sat motionless in front of him, dressed in a fine suit and holding a walking stick. And he had said nothing in his defense.

"Have you anything to say in your defense, Mr. Little?"

"*Pas de tout*," he replied.

"What?"

"Nothing, sheriff. I have nothing to add to this boy's testimony."

Dan Barkin looked around the stilled room.

"Well then I have no choice but to find you guilty in the murder of Judge Abel Durand and his wife Rose O'Keefe Durand. And I order that you will be moved to the county seat in Guthrie tomorrow morning and on the day after that...or however long it takes them to set up the scaffold...you will be hung until you are good and dead."

"In fact, I do have one request Marshall," said John Little.

"Get on with it," said the sheriff.

"I prefer to be hung at night, if that be possible. The night before if you like - I am not asking for no extra time on this earth."

"Strangest guldarn request I never heard," puzzled the Marshall. "Would you mind explaining yourself?"

"I want to be wide awake for my execution. My habit is to wake around noon and it's too damn hot to do a hanging at high noon anyway."

"Reckon it is," said Barkin.

"So I propose to be hung at midnight," said John Little. "Besides, I figure we're close to the full moon anyway and with a little luck everybody should have a grand view."

"This will be the second time I've let you speak out of order."

"So it would, sheriff."

"And I reckon I'm a going to grant your request on a cause of that."

"Therefore I also order that John Little be moved to the county seat at Guthrie and taken from his cell around midnight day after next and hung by the neck until dead. That satisfies you?"

"*Oui.*"

"And stop talking that damn Frenchie talk - gets on my nerves." said the Marshall.

The scaffold had been set at the edge of the town and was the highest structure for miles around, nearly two stories off the ground with a black cloth draping the staging area of death. When they came to get him from his cell, John Little was lying in his cot reading and he asked the Marshall if he might take the book with him up to the scaffold. The Marshall examined the book and found no weapon hidden inside and allowed it.

John Little stood next to the executioner, a friendly sort due to his constant smile but one who never showed his teeth and was rumored to never had made a noose so unwieldy that it took a man's head off. Ironically, the executioner himself had once been the innocent victim of a botched lynching by some cowboys in west Texas over a case of badly branded cattle. The young cowboy who had fixed the noose on him was so nervous that he mistakenly looped the rope around the horn of the saddle before looping it over the low-slung branch of a nearby tree. When they had swatted the horse on his rump the saddle had come flying off and the executioner was left still sitting on suspended saddle with his neck still in tact. The cowboys were so astonished that they let him go, figuring it to be some kind of miracle. Unfortunately for the executioner, when the saddle had ripped off the horse, the horn had bashed right into the mouth, knocking out all his teeth and permanently widening his mouth into a bizarre smile.

Dan Barkin stood on the other side of the scaffold and helped position John Little on the trap door, his arms bound tightly behind him and his ankles as well. The sheriff asked him if he had anything to say and he could only think to quote Walt Whitman:

"Goodbye my Fancy! Farewell, dear mate, dear love! I'm going away, I know not where, or to what fortune, or whether I may ever see you again, so Good-bye my Fancy," he shouted out to the assembled death watchers. "Now for my last - let me look back a moment; The slower fainter ticking of the clock is in me, Exit, nightfall and soon the heart-thud stopping. Long have we lived, joy'd, caress'd together; Delightful! - now separation - Goodbye my Fancy." There was total silence in the crowd as he continued. "Yet let me not be too hasty, Long indeed have we lived, slept, filter'd, become really blended into one; Then if we die we die together, (yes, we'll remain one,) If we go anywhere we'll go together to meet what happens, May-be we'll be better off and blither, and learn something, May-be it is you yourself now really ushering me to the true songs, (who knows?) May-be it is you the mortal knob really undoing, turning – so now finally, Goodbye - and hail! my Fancy."

The crowd stood dumfounded and than broke into spontaneous applause. They had never heard a dying man so eloquent, so entertaining, so clear and fearless with his last testimony. Most folks figured it was John Little's words himself, made up on the spot. Besides, most folks couldn't read a spit and had never heard of Whitman or any other poet anyway.

When the cheering died down, John Little could not resist but adding his final epilogue:

"Have you heard that it was good to gain the day?" he bellowed. "I also say it is good to fall... Battles are lost in the same spirit in which they are won."

Again, the applause was tremendous. After all was this not the hometown boy, the wicked prodigal son, come home again perhaps not to make good, but still to help give a name to Vendee, some now calling it the murder capital of Oklahoma.

But Dan Barkin had had about enough of all this poetry. Just the sound of the words made him nervous. He nodded impatiently to the grinning executioner to get on with his work. Barkin and the executioner stepped back from the spring loaded door and with a deft move the executioner kicked out the latch that held it in place and John Little dropped straight away out of sight like a magician's trick.

He was waiting for the itchy rope to rip his head off and his neck was tensed and his head held way back. A condemned man in Colorado had once told him it was the cleanest way to go. But as he stood there for his last seconds John Little couldn't help but wonder - how did that man know? He was waiting for that final violent twist but the jolt he expected came from far down below, from his feet and on up to his knees. He had landed on somebody's shoulders, with hands grabbing him rightly by the ankles.

"Make like you be dead," the Indian Jack Blankets whispered up to him. And he did.

How the Indian fixed it with the undertaker, draping the gallows and lengthening the rope was something John Little never figured out until he saw that Cherokee squaw, wife of the undertaker, sitting in the back of the coffin makers shop and wrapped grinning in a blanket when he dared to raise his head from under the sheet that had been placed over him. The undertaker's squaw placed her finger to her lips.

"Don't say nothing, dead man," she whispered to him.

The undertaker walked in, clearly agitated, dressed in a rubber apron and throwing his towel down on the coffin.

"Guess they're probably going to hang all of us now," he said. "Seems folks want to exhibit the body out in front of the sheriff's office. They say you're some kind of legend round here." He turned to his Indian wife. "Now you tell me how the hell am I going to do that? You go ask your no good brother Jack Blankets how he's going to fix this one up for me, eh?"

She poked her small husband in the chest. "You use some other white man's body. They all look the same to me anyhow," she replied.

So when the photograph that was published in the Denver Times of "Local man hung in Oklahoma on charge of murdering his mother and stepfather" George O'Keefe nearly fell out of his chair.

"What the hell...?"

He took the newspaper out into the street to get a better look.

"This don't look like Petit Jean to me," he said to no one in particular.

Chapter 14

The boy, twirling drunk, had shot six holes into the tin roof of the north Texas saloon, sending all the patrons scurrying under the tables and was fumbling as he tried to reload, missing the pistol's chambers and scattering bullets all over the floor when the huge bartender snuck up on him from behind, grabbed him and held him still while someone grabbed his gun out of his hands and tossed it on the bar. The bartender finally let the boy go and went behind the bar, tucking the boy's gun into his apron.

"Give me back my Colt, mister. You got no right to take my gun. I ain't shot anybody yet, have I?"

"I'll give you back your gun in the morning when you've slept off what ever kind of a wicked drunk you're on son."

"I ain't drunk. I'm just celebrating."

"Celebrating what? That you shot a hole in my ceiling? Damn thing will probably start leaking now."

"I'm celebrating that I'm gonna be the fellow who killed that famous bastard John Little."

The twenty or so men in the bar became quiet at the mention of the name.

"Are you saying you killed John Little? I didn't hear anything about that," said the bartender.

"Can't you understand English, Mister? I said I'm gonna kill him - didn't say it's done. Just gotta find him first."

"Well, when you do find him, son, I suggest that you don't get into no drinking contest, because I suspect you'll be on the losing end of that competition."

The boy swelled with rage and he felt for his gun, forgetting it had already been taken from him.

"What I suspect I'll do first is accuse him of being a no good murdering bastard coward...and when he goes for his guns I'll shoot him good, you can bet on it."

At this boast nearly all the men in the bar erupted in a burst of laughter before going back to their gambling and whoring.

"Come on over here to the bar, son," said the bartender. "Let me give you some advice."

The boy was aware that he was being laughed at and he stood frozen and transfixed with a rage boiling and rising from his gut. If only I had my gun, he thought, I might just begin shooting some of these bastards right here.

"These folks don't know me," he warned. "When I say I'm a gonna do something, why then I'm sure as..."

"Listen son," interrupted the bartender. "John Little came to this town once and left three men dead at that table right there before they even got a shot off at him, in fact, two of those men didn't even get their guns out of their belts. I don't reckon killing him will be so easy, son. If I was you I'd pick a less advanced target."

"But I got all the time in the world," said the boy. "I'm a hell of a lot younger than he is and I've been following him for nearly three years."

"But do you even know who John Little is? Do you know what he looks like? Do you know how fast he can kill a man?" asked the bartender. "Besides, some folks say the law hung him back in Oklahoma some years ago."

"Yeah, I know what he looks like," said the boy. "I'll never forget his face. And I swear he weren't the man they hung back their in Vendee, Oklahoma."

"And why you never forget face?" Asked the old Indian sitting in the corner and all turned to look at Jack Blankets, huddling by the stove in his worn-out covering. It was the first word the Indian had spoken since entering the place late that afternoon.

The boy strolled over to where the Indian squat on the floor and looked down on him contemptuously.

"I don't need to tell no goddamn Indian nothing about nothing. You understand that?"

There was a long pause. The bartender unsure if he should give the boy back his gun or not in case the old Indian pulled a knife. Of course, the Indian had not caused him or anybody else any trouble, just sitting by the stove enjoying the warmth of the red coals, but he sure as hell didn't want anybody thinking he was soft on Indians. Here in Texas, that could be ruinous for business.

The boy loudly addressed the bar: "I'll be damned if I'm gonna sit here and watch some redskin butting into white men's business here.

196

What kind of town is this anyway?"

Nobody in the bar liked this boy, hardly a man, who could have killed someone with his crazy shooting but then again nobody was about to stand up for the Indians after all the terrible things they'd done, even if nobody was really sure exactly what those terrible things were.

Jack Blankets broke the silence. "I understand," he said. "I speak too much for my own good." And he ducked his head back into his blanket.

The bartender turned toward the boy. "Now what be your name son? So when I hear John Little is finally laid in the ground, I can say I personally knew the man who done it."

"Durand," said the boy. "Robert E. Durand."

It was the rhythm of those hooves, lopsided and unfaltering that always led him back to his poetry. On long rides he would hold the book open in front of him and force himself to memorize long passages. Often, on a deserted prairie trail he found himself as alone as a man could be and he would stand high in his stirrups, his hands extended toward the heavens and chant: "I celebrate myself."

A passing group of renegade Kiowa who had trailed him for a day and half and were considering stealing his horse and scalping him, changed their mind after agreeing among themselves that this white man must be crazy and it would certainly be very bad medicine to harm him; best to leave him alone talking to the sky like that and so they let him ride on unmolested.

John Little didn't care for sleeping out of doors. All the goose feather pillows at Uncle George's whorehouse in Manhattan had instilled a life long addiction to the comforts of a soft bed and a well-sealed roof over his head. But as distances were far and travel was as much a part of his business as shooting was, he had grown accustomed to sleeping under the stars or rain or snow during his journeys. Once he had found a rattler curled right up next to him half under his blanket and had managed to move ever so slowly out of his sleeping roll so as not to disturb it. Then he took out his Winchester and blew its head off and left the blanket where it lay covered with the bloody fragments.

But this night the weather was fine and John Little decided to camp in the open end of a canyon, under a low, luminous full moon that he could read his books by. He had gathered enough dry wood to keep a low fire cooking to keep the coyotes from pissing on his gear during the night, and he fell asleep just after darkness fell, first having re-read a Ned Buntline's history of Wild Bill Hickok even while knowing it was about as close to the truth as he was to China. But he imagined that just to earn the nickname of "Wild" out in the west was not something a fellow came by easy, a man having to be fairly *wild* just to make the trek out here – and women even more so.

Of course, Hickok had been renowned for his adept handling of Indians and card cheats alike. They say his murder was due to an unlucky hand of cards and being caught with his back against the door but John Little figured it was more likely he had actually been hiding his well known face from the throng of revenge seekers who might blow him away at any given moment. But Hickok had put Deadwood on the map, and that was where John Little was headed.

He eyes popped open at a scraping sound in the brush; something was moving towards him, getting closer and his grip tightened around the Remington under his blanket. John figured he might shoot himself in the leg some morning if his nerves were too much on edge but he was willing to take that chance rather than be bushwhacked in the middle of nowhere with his guns out of reach. He too, like Hickok, entertained a host of revenge seekers: the kin of killers he'd put in their graves or just young toughs who would love nothing better than to blow him to kingdom come, merely to enhance their own reputations.

Not wanting to startle the intruder into blasting him while he still lay in his blanket, John lay still and continued the sound of his steady snoring, keeping one eye barely open enough to see a small dark figure approaching, no gun in sight and bending low, just inches from his face when John Little pulled out his Remington from under his blanket and stuck it in the intruder's face.

"*Bon Soir*, stranger," he said. "Just keep your hands up where I can see them and walk back toward the fire there."

The intruder said nothing and obeyed; dressed in a long brown duster, and a hat so big it covered half his face.

"Now take off that tent you call a hat," said John Little.

The stranger complied and John Little could see his would be attacker was really no more than a boy - maybe sixteen years old – whose uncombed blond hair seemed to be cut with a bowl around his head and whose face sported a wispy moustache.

"Want me to turn around so you can shoot me in the back?" said the boy arrogantly.

"No," said John Little. "I think, *ce soir* I prefer to shoot you in the gut and watch you roll around the fire for a while. I was getting kind of bored anyway, since that moon set and it being too dark now for reading."

That shut the boy up for a moment, his eyes wide. Finally he spoke: "You know I could have done you in myself too, while you were sleeping in your blankets there, but I'm an honorable man."

"Well, I suppose if you would have decided to take such a imbecilic action you might have had to cock your pistol first and I tell you something, I've got the queerest habit: whenever I hear a pistol click I always let off a few shots in that direction just for old times' sake."

"Old times sake?"

"Yeah, old times' sake, guess I'm sentimental for those two Mormons I had to bury over in Utah under the prettiest moon you ever could imagine. And I didn't know one damn Mormon song to sing to them boys, but they had the damndest loudest clicking pistols I ever heard in my life - Mon Dieu – like chopping logs for a fire. I apologized for shooting them and spoiling all their fun as they lay dying, but I figured they had come to do the same to me anyway so *chacun son tour*, eh?"

"What?" said the boy.

"Oh...everybody gets their turn, I reckon." He sat up and put his pistol back in its holster. "You just stay put there by the fire with your hands on your head, son, while I fix us some coffee."

"How do you know I won't pull out my gun?"

"I'm hoping you will," said John Little. "So I can get back to sleep. I got a hell of a journey ahead of me."

He walked to the fire and put the coffee pot back between two rocks over the still glowing coals and fetched two cups from his saddlebags. In a minute the coffee was hissing and he gave the boy a cup.

"So what'd you wake me up for son? You lonely for some conversation out here in the prairie?"

"Can I talk now?" said the boy.

"French or English," said John Little. "Take your pick."

"I been following you for a few years now" said the boy. "I arrived in Denver the day after you left and I set out after you."

"You have some business with me, son?"

"You might say that."

"And what would that be."

"I'm the man whose gonna kill you, John Little," he said with eyes full of rage. "You can count on it!"

John Little took the coffee from his mouth. "Mais oui? Figure your reputation needs a little boost? Aim to be a gunslinger yourself? Let me tell you something son, there are plenty of men out there who might get the drop on me but you aren't one of them. At least not until you learn to tread a little lighter out here on the range."

"You killed my Daddy," said the boy. "In cold blood."

"I ain't never killed anyone in cold blood," said John Little. "Every man I laid in his grave I gave a fighting chance. Nothing more than self defense"

"His name was Durand, just like me, and you shot him pointblank while he was sleeping." Said the boy. "I saw you with my own eyes."

John Little said nothing. Then he threw the coffee into the fire and walked over to the boy who was visibly trembling but still not backing down. He studied the boys face and, yes, he could see the traces of Durand: arrogance in the down-turned mouth, the same wavy hair, and the same cold, steel-blue eyes.

"What do you know about me killing Abel Durand? You heard that from someone?"

"I was there, I tell you. I know that you snuck in his room pretending to be a priest one night and you shot an unarmed man although nobody believed me."

"Your daddy turned out to be not so unarmed that night...it was something I had to do. Him and his man set up my own daddy and shot him dead. Had to be done before I could get on with my life. Don't suppose I owe any man an explanation - no one ever gave me none - but I didn't know Durand had a son...not that it would have made a whole lot of difference, I imagine."

"Your drunken father was killed in a fair fight over a game of cards, holding his own gun in his hand outright. He weren't murdered."

"It weren't no fair fight," said John Little. "I was there."

"I can't stand to look at you," said the boy. "Either you kill me or let me go. But I'll be back."

"*Comme tu veux*, you can go as you please. But the next time you try and get the drop on me in the middle of the night you won't be leaving under your own walking power, I can tell you that."

The boy got up and walked to the edge of the brush where he mounted his horse. John Little was standing now and watched him. "Boy, who told you that nonsense about it being a fair fight?"

"My mother told me," said the boy as he hooked a boot in the stirrup. "And she knew both men."

"Who is your mother?"

"Rose," said the boy. "Rose Durand," and he mounted his horse and turned to face John Little: "Damn you!" screamed the boy. "You self puffing son of a bitch. I'll kill you someday - you can be sure of that. You'll wish you been caught by Comanches after I'm through with you. Your kinfolk won't recognize you either I swear. I swear to you Robert E. Durand will avenge his father's murder. That's a promise!"

"Murderer," he screamed and the canyon echoed his words as he ran off into the darkness.

John Little stood motionless, his stinging eyes squinting after the boy until all was quiet again. He sat for a long time by the dwindling coals of his fire totally motionless, staring into the void, unable to read and therefore, unable to think.

Finally, he walked to his saddlebags and took out his copy of Whitman's Leaves of Grass and read until the sun came up.

Chapter 15

When John Little first crossed Theodore Roosevelt in the *Badlands* of the Dakota Territory, Teddy was just another rich easterner looking for thrills on the open range. Ironically, both men had been looking for the same pair of rustlers - brothers by the name of Rodson – and Teddy and his noble friend the Marquis de Mores had formed a semi-official posse on behalf of the citizens of a Black Hills town. John Little was working for a stockman's association farther south and had tracked the men further and further north, getting more and more irritated as the weather turned sour and hoping he might come across the men in a town, preferring to do his killing on the streets or in a saloon, close to his hotel. The stockmen were rich, having grabbed up the best land for themselves and driving most of the sheepherders west to Utah. They could pay John Little what he asked for and more but he had decided that this would be the last set of rustlers that he would take on to eliminate for anybody. The conditions were always dreadfully poor, days and days of riding and tracking and there was no sport in it; rustlers most often being cowboys gone bad who couldn't shoot worth a nickel. Besides, now he had heard that the notorious Rodson brothers were just out of luck settlers and family men with a hungry batch of kids, not hard-core thieves. Only luckless tenant farmers fallen on rough times.

He found the two men easily one evening; they were drunk and sitting in front of a blazing fire and he quickly subdued them, tying them to each other and trying to decide whether to kill them on the spot or bring them in for a quick trial and let the stockman have the thrill of hanging them and attaching signs around their necks announcing *This is what we do to rustlers*. In fact, killing them seemed to be the charitable thing to do. No need to subject their children to the sight of them spinning in the air with a rope around their necks as the law was unbending in these parts: you steal cows or horses and you hang. John was sitting there looking at his two captives, now passed out and sleeping, and trying to decide what to do when Teddy Roosevelt and his bunch arrived. The posse, mostly consisting of second-rate cowboys who had fallen into a cushy spell of hunting with a rich easterner, rode into the campground with as much stealth as a herd of buffalos.

"We've got them, men!" Cried Teddy to his boys as he nearly fell off his horse. "Dismount and take cover!"

John Little stood up, his guns at his side, watching as this strange little man with a bearskin hat, gold rimmed glasses and a panther's gnarly smile, approached him.

"And who be you with these two varmints?" Teddy asked, sputtering into his face. John Little knew who Teddy Roosevelt was; news traveled fast in these parts of the wealthy New Yorker who had lost his young wife to disease back east and was trying to assuage his grief by playing cowboy for a while, trying to pick up the rough lingo of the ranch hands he hung around with, being not very talented at anything in particular besides talking. His riding or shooting was nothing to write home about but still he had a certain gutsy-ness and fortitude that the cowboys grudgingly respected.

"Who be I?" asked John Little. "I guess I be the man who's going to take these two *varmints* back to Deadwood for trial. And whom, might I ask, be you?"

"Name's Theodore Roosevelt but everyone calls me Teddy on account of those bear cubs I captured." He went on in his rapid-fire speech. "Kind of stuck with me and I like it. Has a certain flair I enjoy."

"You captured bear cubs?" asked John Little. "All by yourself? Sounds like quite a dangerous feat."

At that moment a member of Teddy's posse came over to loudly explain that the man Teddy was addressing was a well known killer of men all over the west, not a man to rile and perhaps it be best if they just let him take these men back to Deadwood and be on their way safely back to Teddy's ranch nestled in the black hills.

Teddy listened to the man and sized up John Little, who stood in front of him, bemused at the power of his reputation on his posse. But Teddy was not happy with this turn of events. He had set out to capture these rustlers and did not want to return empty handed, with the attendant loss of face.

"Would you consider turning these men over to us, sir?" Teddy asked John Little. "I could pay you the reward, myself. We are perhaps better equipped than one man alone out here in the field to guarantee their safe return. These hombres might have cohorts waiting in ambush somewhere along the trail. Could be dangerous."

"I think I'll be OK," said John Little. "No more bear cubs left around here waiting to attack. Reckon you wiped them all out in ferocious hand to hand combat."

Teddy pondered the situation for a moment, trying to make the best face in front of his men. "Well, Mr. Little, do you have any objections if we accompany you back to Deadwood when you turn these men over to the rightful authorities? There's safety in numbers, you know. A man can't be too careful in these parts."

John Little shook his head and regarded the bespectacled little man who had taken no risk in capturing these men, and now wanted to be part of the glory of turning them in and he laughed.

"You should be a politician, sir," he said. "I'll tell you what, if you've got any books in your gear there that I might read on the way, you can ride along to your heart's content."

"Bully!" Yelled Roosevelt. "Someone fetch my library!"

They took their time traveling back to Deadwood and John got to know Teddy Roosevelt, who was as talkative a man as he had ever met. From his time spent in Manhattan he was familiar with many of the New York references that peppered Teddy's speech. And indeed, Teddy had saddlebags full of books that John Little read voraciously, the majority of which were about a fictional west, full of wild cowboys, brave Indian scouts and fearsome bad-men, all written by easterners. But Teddy did have some fine poetry and philosophy books in there as well, and if there

208

was an uncovered night sky and a strong light from the moon, John would stay up late into the night devouring Emerson or Thoreau or Shakespeare.

"So what brought you to this territory in the first place, Mr. Little?" asked Teddy.

"Can't rightly say. I was born in Old Oklahoma and then shipped east when I was a child, and I guess like a homing pigeon I found my way back here. And you?"

"Oh, the adventure of it all, man! And to see it before it disappears."

"What you mean by that?" John Little said with a yawn.

"These great free ranches with their barbarous surroundings are just a primitive stage of man's existence out here in the wilds, I imagine. They will pass away before the onward march of our people. And we who have felt the charm of the life and have exulted in its abounding bigness and its bold restless freedom will not only regret its passing for our own sakes only, but must also feel real sorrow that those who come after us are not to see, as we have seen, what is perhaps the pleasant and healthiest and most exiting phase of American existence. Don't you agree Mr. Little?"

And then Teddy Roosevelt realized that John Little was soundly asleep.

The next night John Little was up late reading Plato when one of the Rodson brothers called him over.

"Hey Mister Little, can I talk to you just for a minute? I got something I want to say to you."

John Little put his book down and walked over to the two rustlers, still securely tied together although the younger one was sleeping, his head resting on his brother's shoulder.

"I got a deal for you mister," said the one who was awake.

"Don't look to me like you're in a position to broker any deals," said John Little.

The rustler nodded toward the sleeping figure. "Cal, here, well, he's my younger brother. It weren't his idea to get into this business. I was stealing them steers by myself for a long time before I talked him into joining me."

"Then that was his mistake," said John Little

"Well, maybe you can call it that, mister. A mistake. And God knows a man has got to pay grievously for his trespasses in these parts. I know that for sure and I'd be a fool to be saying anything against it – laws the law. Reckon if I were you I'd be bringing us in as well. But maybe there's something else to chew on, when a man's got a wife, just barely eighteen years old and newly arrived from Missouri, like my brother Cal here has, and them with two kids with nothing to eat and another one on the way, and when he sees a chance to feed his family by rustling a few steers, well, I don't know if you can call that no crime, mister."

"What are you getting at?"

"Look mister, I know I'm gonna swing for what I done and I don't hold you no grudge for that. You do your job and caught us fair and square and so be it. But how's about letting my brother Cal off and I'll take the rope for both of us?"

"Can't do that," said John Little. "I was paid to bring in both of you men and that's what I aim to do."

"Well, I know these here rich ranchers you're working for and I know what they want most is their damn cattle back. Now I tell you, I got three hundred head hidden way back in one of these here canyons just a days ride from where we are now, and if both of us swing then I'll be damned if those cursed ranchers will ever get those cows back again. Winter's coming and them steers is gonna starve before any cowboy finds 'em the way I got 'em hid."

"*Allors*? What are you saying?"

"I'm saying you take my brother Cal here and a few of these here cowboys and you go pick up those cows and once you do, well, you let my brother go and I promise you, you'll never be hearing from him again, and I'll take our little talk here with me to the grave and meet my maker knowing I did the right thing by my little brother here. I haven't got any kids, lost my only baby to the fever last winter and my wife's about had it with me anyway. I won't be leaving much here on this earth that I'm especially gonna miss."

"I'll think it over," said John Little. "And you keep your mouth shut."

Next morning John spoke to Teddy Roosevelt, asking to loan him two of his best cowboys. As promised, after two days ride, the younger brother led them to a hidden canyon, blocked off by heavy brush and

211

tumbleweed on one end, where over three hundred cows had already grazed on most everything in sight. The cowboys herded the steers and they began to move them out. That night, while the cowboys were sleeping, John Little approached the younger brother and untied him."

"You best leave the territory, *tres vite*."

"What?"

"Fast I said! Get moving as far west as you can go. Then get word to your wife to join you and never come back here. I see your face again in these parts and I'll kill you without a word. And if I hear you tell anybody that John Little let you go scott free, then rest assured that I'll come looking for you and I will kill you when I find you, *comprenez*?"

"You're letting me go, mister?" He asked dumfounded.

"No need to thank me - you can thank your brother. And say a prayer for him as well 'cause he isn't coming with you," said John Little. "Now, I'm going over there to read some Shakespeare and by the time I finish Hamlet's soliloquy I want to turn around and wonder where the hell you gone to."

It was the only time John Little let a man go in his life.

Chapter 16

John Little had nothing against the Spaniards. He'd killed a few Mexicans in his time but you couldn't really call them Spaniards. In half a century the U.S. Cavalry had killed off most of the Indians worth fighting, the Plains tribes nearly out-maneuvering many of the Union's best generals on the battlefield before disease and the repeating rifle made the odds sadly ridiculous and the great chiefs were either dead or so old that getting up the energy for a ghost dance was about all they could manage. Besides, Indian fighting didn't make for good press anymore, revenge for Custer's massacre having lost its zest and popular appeal in local gazettes. But a battleship, sitting in Havana harbor, blown to smithereens by a treacherous Spanish bomb, well, that was a cause for every newspaper in America to fly a huge *"WAR"* banner across their headlines.

Teddy Roosevelt had sent a telegram to John Little in Denver, saying war was just like any other killing for hire job, only this time the travel was longer and the pay a lot worse. Whether out of some sense of patriotism instilled by his father or just plane boredom he went.

One of two things happen when one man saves another's life: there can be an indebtedness that binds the two men together for life, one full of gratitude and the other's esteem risen to that lofty place of saints and saviors. Or there is the other possibility, wherein the man who has been saved must now face not only the frightening specter of his own immortality and even worse his mortal lack of power and will in the face

213

of terror, and he finds he can no longer stand the sight of the man to whom he owes his life. And that is what happened between Little John and Teddy Roosevelt in Cuba.

When the brief Cuban campaign of the Spanish-American War was over, Teddy Roosevelt brought his *Rough Riders* amid much hoopla back to America via Montauk, on the tip of Long Island to their original training grounds at Deep Hollow Ranch. Through his oratory he continued to serve the cause of William Randolph Hearst whose yellow journalism had been the catalyst for the timely war against Spain in the first place although no one imagined that the pale yellow color of the newsprint would get people's attention and live on in journalistic infamy. But the final result was that America for the first time in its history was now a colonial power with its newly conquered islands of Cuba, Puerto Rico and the Philippines, and Teddy was launching his own national political career as San Juan Hill's answer to Vicksburg's Ulysses S. Grant. The whole wide world was to be the next new frontier, there being nothing but dead or debilitated Indians lying out on the old one and with the numerous sugar plantations of Cuba soon to be taken over by rich American consortiums, whose profits would soon start trickling down into the deep pockets of many a congressman in Washington, or at least of those who had supported the war. Ironically, Admiral Dewey's U.S. Naval flotilla finally steamed into Manila harbor when the war was already over, but America was late into the colonial game already, so it made no difference. And such details did little to dissuade the Federal powers that

214

won these islands under the new banner of the American Century from the sacred belief of a manifest destiny gone global. That destiny had led the country in one big skip and jump from the Pacific shores of California to the jungles of the Philippine Islands.

Things grew testy between the ex-district attorney of New York City and John Little once they disembarked back on Montauk, Long Island, itself not too far from Rose O'Keefe's place of birth in Huntington. One of Teddy's other *Rough Riders*, a cowhand from Wyoming named Jenkins, happened to pass on the latest issue of the New York Herald to John Little with the admonition that "I wouldn't read this, partner, if you don't want to get shooting mad at our fearless leader over there."

To John Little's dismay he began to read a very colorful and nearly fictional account of the battle for San Juan Hill where he had been just weeks before; of how Teddy Roosevelt had rallied his troops and led them unafraid charging up the hill on horseback while sniper bullets whizzed past him. The problem was that all the men who fought in the battle remembered very well that for the most part Teddy was lying at the foot of the hill yelling nonsensical commands and waving his saber in the air while cursing his sprained ankle swollen to the size of a coconut. And if it weren't for John Little's deadeye shot into the forehead of a Spanish sniper who launched his own one man assault while perched in a palm tree, today's Herald would instead be full of Teddy Roosevelt's short obituary.

The reporters who were gathered at the train station for the *bully bully*

215

send off of Theodore Roosevelt back down to Washington, watched in awe as Teddy discharged his troops while giving each man a small bonus pay out of his own pocket as well as being allowed to keep their horses. John Little handed the money back to Roosevelt without saying a word and left before the ceremony was through, having sent his own horses out to Colorado by freight train, and headed over to Huntington Harbor in search of family and poetry, anything with a bit of truth in it to get the false taste of politics out of his mouth.

Walt Whitman stood in front of the candy store on the main street of Huntington Harbor admiring a bouquet of red and white candy canes sitting upright in a large glass jar. The proprietress of the store, an old spinster dressed in black, was eyeing him warily as he had been standing nearly motionless in front of the red and white stalks while three crowds of children had pushed ahead of him to buy penny whistles and molasses cookies. Twice now she had asked Whitman if he needed help.

"No, thank you ma'am, I'm just admiring the assortment of sundries available in your store. It is with immense pleasure that I return to the place of my formative years and…"

Then he stopped talking, his eyes went glassy and a look of utmost horror gripped his face. The woman, who was waiting politely for him to finish, finally backed away and went looking for someone to help her with this strange man who was having some kind of a fit in her store.

Whitman had been looking at the candy canes, the red and the white stripes twirling up the stalks, when there was a booming noise from down

216

the street, probably a thunderous closing of a warehouse door or a horse kicking a stall. All at once he was psychically jolted back in time to the Civil War field hospitals and again he envisioned wounded young soldiers losing legs and arms without aid of anesthesia, their own bloody stalks, red and white like candy canes, lying in a pile in the back of the hospital.

After his brother was wounded at Fredericksburg, Whitman had traveled to the heart of the war to care for him and soon found himself doing the rounds of the huge Union hospitals in Washington, where 50,000 wounded lay in the most unsanitary of conditions. Soon he was a regular fixture, strolling from cot to cot with a basket or haversack on his arm as the soldiers called out his name. He dispensed fruits, cakes and candy, pipes and tobacco, pens and sheets of paper or postage stamps, and he often wrote letters home for those unable to do it for themselves. When it was time for him to leave voices would call out after him: "Walt, Walt, come again! Come again!"

After the war, Whitman settled in New Jersey in the industrial town of Camden with his brother George. But he often came back to Long Island, unannounced and incognito, as if anybody really cared, to roam the docks and the beaches of Huntington while composing verse in his head. He wore so many hats that at times it could get confusing as to exactly who the real Walt Whitman was. In addition to composing verse, under another name he was also writing critiques of his own books of poetry for a Brooklyn paper. No matter, he was his own greatest fan, and if the world was slow to catch on, he would, indeed, celebrate himself.

Whitman found the Wagram tavern much as he had remembered: a smoky place with sailors playing cards, biding their time until sailing off for more whaling or just hauling freight to other ports along the Eastern seaboard. Of course, Father Wagram had aged plenty; his once strong back now stooped but he was still a formidable presence behind the bar and even in his advanced age was capable of breaking up fights between strong, drunk sailors.

When John Little strolled in the tavern himself, still wearing his tan *Rough Riders* uniform, but without the stiff brimmed expeditionary hat that was useless on horseback, catching the wind and blowing off of his head. He thought of his father, John O'Keefe, who had strolled into the same tavern after another war and then left with his mother for the great western adventure and now them both lying dead and buried behind the Vendee Church of Saint Mary. John Little had never met his grandfather and he supposed it must be the skinny old man with the long gray beard staring into the fire.

"Excuse me sir, but you be *Monsieur* Wagram then?" He asked.

Whitman looked at him a long time before replying.

"You remind me of somebody, sir. A long time ago..."

"Then I suppose you are the gentlemen I'm looking for," said John Little. "You are father Wagram?"

"No, it's not me, it's that burly looking old fellow behind the bar with the white apron. I'm sure that would be the father Wagram you're looking for."

John Little started to walk away when Whitman called him back.

"It was a girl, a beautiful girl who played with hoops, and helped her mama with the cooking. She had your eyes, before the war, I believe."

"Excuse me, sir?" said John Little, thinking the man drunk or deranged, the long gray beard having transformed Whitman from the clean shaven poet he had met so many years ago. He didn't recognize him at all. "I best be getting on my way."

He strolled to the bar to see his grandfather busily washing and drying glasses behind the counter.

"Father Wagram?" he asked.

"Oui, its me if that's who you be looking for. *Bon Jour monsieur.*"

"Jean Wagram?"

"Yes, sir. And now if you'll excuse me I've got to..."

"It's, uh...Petit Jean, sir. Your grandson."

The old man dropped the glass to the floor and it shattered. The barroom was quiet and Walt Whitman stood up by the fireplace and said softly to himself. "Ah yes, it was the girl, the daughter, who once worked here. It was her eyes that I saw so clearly. She must of had a son," and hastily took out a piece of paper and an oft sharpened stub of pencil and began to scribble.

It is not to diffuse you that you were born of your mother and father... he looked over at the two men who were now embraced, tears in the older man's eyes. *It is to identify you.* He scribbled on and on, crossing out words and lines until finally writing, *The law of the past cannot be eluded, the law of the present and future cannot be eluded. The law of the living cannot be eluded...it is eternal.'*

Then Whitman put away his notebook and walked out of the tavern to board his coach back to New Jersey.

Chapter 17

When John Little returned to Denver, a telegram was waiting for him and he knew he must go now, and not think about not going and he only began to doubt himself when he stood at the far side of the short street that went through town and turned briefly to face his own house.

"The past is the only thing that lasts," he whispered to himself.

It was seven o'clock on a Sunday morning with a church bell ringing loudly down at the more proper end of town, but on this side the saloon was already full of drunken cowboys and there was music wafting down the street. The dust of the road lifted easily as he scraped his injured leg along behind him, a wet spot on his boot where the blood soaked through. When Robert E. Durand had come bursting out of the saloon firing his guns wildly, a bullet had caught John Little in the leg, knocking him off his feet, but he was quickly rolling on the ground with a Remington 44 cocked in his hand, quickly firing off two shots aimed low. He didn't want to kill Robert E. Durand, but with the boy continuing to shoot at him like that he knew he'd have no choice. John Little shot him once in the groin, aiming for his thigh, and the boy bent over in pain but kept firing nonetheless. The second bullet caught the boy right at the top of his stomach, knocking him off his legs and landing senseless on the steps to the saloon door, his two guns still gripped in his hands. Just for a moment there was a eerie silence on the street, men peering out from behind tables and chairs in the saloon and the churchgoing crowd at the other end of the street huddling to protect their children from stray gunfire. John Little moved as fast as he could to where the boy had fallen.

The Durand boy was deathly pale, holding both hands to his stomach. "Oh my god! Oh my god!" he cried over and over. John Little pulled up the boy's shirt and knew there was nothing any doctor could do for him. Standing over him now, in the bright Sunday morning light, John Little was stunned to see how young the boy really was, with a wispy moustache and still freckled face. He held the boy close to him. At first he was speechless but with the boy staring and groaning in pain he searched for some useless words to comfort him.

"Don't worry, son. The doc here in town is going to patch you up. You put up a fine fight. No man twice your age could have done more. You just try to relax now, son - no need to say anything more."

But as he spoke John Little saw the boy drifting away. One eye was closed and there was a trickle of blood coming from his mouth and nose and, more ominously, the blood was literally gushing out of the wound in the boy's stomach, soaking the wooden sidewalk and dripping down the stairs into the dusty street. He would be dead before any doctor arrived. Robert E. Durand moved one hand in front of him and feebly grabbed John Little by the collar of his coat, trying to pull him close to him.

"Confession," he said. "Take my confession. Save me from Hell…"

"I ain't no priest, son…" but Robert E. Durand started talking and crossing himself and saying the centuries old ritual and then he stopped in the middle of a word, his mouth still open, left behind, suspended as this life, this day, moved forever past without him. John Little shut the boy's eyes with his fingertips and laid him down with his head resting on the steps, folding his arms across his chest. He reached for the boy's hat, shapeless and dirty, nothing a man would wear, and covered the boy's face.

The boy was dead now and John Little limped down the street to find a carpenter or undertaker, to make a coffin. His own wounds needed attention but that could wait. When he returned with the carpenter, his nightshirt still hanging out of his pants, everyone in the saloon had poured out into the street and two cowboys were holding Robert E. Durand's stiffening body, propped against the wall while someone posed the boy's arms across his chest with his guns still gripped in his hands. A crude wooden sign, "Kilt by the famous gunman - John Little," was hung around the boy's neck with fence wire. A photographer was setting up his tripod in front of the body about to explode lighting powder to illuminate his photograph.

John Little pushed through the crowd to where the boy's lifeless body stood, a white kerchief tied tightly on his leg stemming the flow of blood where the boy had shot him. The bullet had gone clear through the fleshy part of his calf, it hurt like hell but he knew it would be all right. He grimaced as he walked over to view Robert E. Durand's body: with the boys eyes shut his age was even more noticeable. John Little stood in front of the corpse and there was quiet all around. Usually at such a moment, a crowd of townsfolk might be cheering him or buying free drinks all around if he had finally lain to rest a local badman who had been terrorizing law-abiding citizens, but not this time. Robert E. Durand was barely out of short pants. And now his life was over.

Finally someone spoke: it was the photographer asking if he would mind posing in front of the body. John Little looked at the photographer for a minute and then drew his gun and shot the camera cleanly right through the lens, which sent the crowd scurrying for cover as he turned and walked away from them up toward the hotel.

Chapter 18

Although the open sky overhead was clear, he dreamed he was a boy again back in his straw bed in the farmhouse of Vendee during a terrible storm. The tempest was furious and kept bashing a small window above his bed open and he was trying to wedge something into the window jam to force it shut.

"That won't do," said his father's voice. "That wind will never stop blowing."

"But where did you go?" Asked the boy.

"Dead is just a word for the living," said his father. "It really doesn't apply to my current situation. I just stopped off somewhere down the road, that's all. Now I dropped by to say hello, son."

"I held your head in my arms...you said...you were sorry..."

"What I'm really sorry about is you," said his father. "You're an outlaw and a killer now and it's my fault, I suppose."

"It ain't anybodies fault what I am and I don't break no laws. *Mon Dieu*, are you alive or...am I dead?"

"Alive, it's a funny word as well," said his father. "I'm just here that's all. I came by to tell you a few things."

"Like what things? And why haven't you grown? You look the same as the day you were shot?"

"Even got the same bullet hole," John O'Keefe pulled up his white shirt to reveal a large festering wound. "Won't go away, I don't know why.

225

But I've grown use to it."

"I guess you can grow used to anything."

"But you've grown far too used to killing and its got to stop, son. I didn't bring no killer into this world."

"Well I suppose you did, all right. Or are all those men I put in the ground going to come back to lecture me as well? Reckon it's a waste of time."

"The only one you really hated with any sense of passion is still walking this earth."

"Who might that be?"

"Judge Durand,"

"I laid him out with your own derringer."

"That gun never could shoot worth a damn. You just exploded some black powder into the man's ear - that's all. I suspect his hearing didn't improve because of it."

"You mean he's alive,"

"I didn't say that. Is a man dead if he lives on in the tortured soul of another?"

"You speak in riddles,"

"Don't you think it's a wonder I speak at all, son?"

"So what else you got to deal with me besides to stop killing?"

With that the apparition grew large and ominous, hovering over John Little, both darkening the room and emitting a terrifying light and a sulphurous steely smell.

"Get my family back together!" he bellowed. "Go find your sister and drag her from the gutter where she lives. And find my wife..." the apparition began to cry, to bellow, to howl with all the sadness of a lonely ghost. "And damn her bottles!"

And then he was gone and the wind was still howling. John Little lay back in his bed and amazedly enough he began to fall back into sleep easily, to soothing dreams and to smile under his moustache.

The next morning, the sight in front of him was fantastic, unbelievable to a man, but his horse continued to lope along as if nothing had changed. A rainbow crossed the valley in front of him like something out of a fairly tale – and arched from peak to peak. John Little let his reins fall and stared at the vision in front of him before something forced him off his horse to the ground and onto his knees. Now the rainbow was widening and doubling upon itself until it seemed to engulf the whole sky in a prism, a sea of colors, reds to yellows to greens and purples in between. At first, John Little thought this must be what death looks like or he had eaten something rotten and then he heard a voice that spoke in no language he had ever known. Not French nor English but just the sounds and the cooing of words and it caressed him and comforted him better than any words ever could and, instinctively, he knew what the voice meant and that he would follow its admonitions and he took off his gun belt and left it in the sandy trail in between the prints of his horses hoof and continued on his way home.

This was the release he had been waiting for, sweet as a brown paper bag full of candy that he had wolfed down as a boy. How many men had he killed to avenge his father? It was difficult to count but now he was rich and famous and it was on account of it, on account of this tragedy that had marked him and honed his ability to use guns to kill men.

"I'm through, Qwing So," he said shortly after entering his house. "No more guns."

"You always hang up your guns," she said continuing to clean, to dust, to examine a chipped vase brought from China by one of her sisters now gone even further west, working the railroad men, overcome with Syphilis and worse.

"No, its for real this time. Those Remingtons are gone from our life, dropped in the dust. I don't want that life no more. *C'est fini.*"

"You never did like it, you hate to travel, to pack."

"Its not the travel I'm talking about. *Mon Dieu* woman! Something awesome has happened to me."

Qwing So put down her dusting and sat in the straight-backed chair next to John Little who stared into the unlit fireplace.

"What happened? Are you hurt?"

"No I ain't hurt...I saw a rainbow."

"It weren't the first, I'm sure,"

"No...but I don't want it to be the last either."

She knew what he meant. "What'll you do? Go work for your Uncle?"

"No, tending whores is not for me. I thought I might...build a church...work in it or something."

Qwing So got right off her chair and placed her soft yellow white wrist on his forehead. No, he was cool. She was relieved; afraid it might be the cholera.

"But John Little, you know a priest can't be married."

"I don't aim to be no goddamn priest. I just aim to build a church."

And that he did. He built a glorious white church in the center of town. He bought Harding's stable and then to everybody's surprise just tore the whole shebang down in a pile of dust and boards, sold off the horses and kept building his church until he had the highest steeple in the territory. He painted it white and kept putting coats of paint on the building until it nearly shone like a beacon at night, with a gloss as high as moustache wax. Finally, he added the most beautiful, the most melodic set of brass bells ordered from a St. Louis foundry on top of the steeple and he rang them profusely, three times a day, morning, noon and night.

But he wouldn't open the doors to his church, nor put a cross atop its steeple, nor bibles in its pews. Just a simple sign out front proclaiming "The Little Church - All Welcome" although in fact nobody really was, yet.

The priest had been riding for close to three months on that mule, slowly making progress up from Arizona to Oklahoma and finally across to Colorado and when he arrived, caked in dust with his feet hanging off the side of that wretched animal, he looked less like a priest than just another luckless prospector. He parked his mule in front of the saloon, not bothering to tie it up, walked in and ordered a whisky.

Recognizing him as a priest, the bartender regarded him strangely: "We don't get many men of the cloth in here. Makes the girls upstairs feel kind of...indecent in front of God, if you know what I mean. They tend to dress rather informally."

"Let them come to me however they be, whatever they got on," said Father Bachet. "I'm a priest with no church and my God has all but abandoned me. Cast me out in the wilderness with nothing but naked savages and cactus and the blistering sun. What your girls do with their shameful prize makes not a damn bit of difference to me. And what about that whisky?"

"Coming up," said the Bartender. He yelled up the stairs: "Nell! Tell them girls of yours they can quit being spooked - this isn't no Roman priest in here, just another thirsty man, I reckon."

Slowly the girls began to appear out of their doorways, like timid puppies, dressed in nightgowns of silk and cotton with only shawls to keep them warm. "I don't care if he is no priest or not," said one of them. "I am not bringing no man dressed in black with a little white collar into my bed. I've got enough sinning on my soul already thank you very much."

Father Bachet spent all of that day and most of the next in the bar refusing to leave and bedding any of those girls that would have him in his disheveled state. Finally he got up the nerve or was drunk enough to ask

230

someone to fetch John Little, who came right down from his church.

"I know you must hate me and I fear you're going to kill me," he said. "But nevertheless I have been searching for you and my absolution as if they stood together. Whatever you do, I just ask your forgiveness, that's all."

"I don't know what you're talking about. I don't even know you." John Little looked at the drunken little man, unshaven, his pants undone.

The priest dropped to his knees. "I'm the one who sent you back east when you were a boy. I'm the one who helped Judge Durand take your daddy's farm, and I'm the one who..." But he couldn't go on and he broke down sobbing.

"Father Bachet?" Said John Little stunned. "What in hell happened to you?"

"That's just it," said the priest trying to control his crying. "I got caught in the currents of hell, I did. I thought I was following the Lord but I was only following the power and the glory of my own pride and look where it has taken me, look what it has done to me, this cursed self-contentment of mine." Again, he began to whimper and tears filled his eyes. "I have buggered Indian women until they sent me away disgusted. And I have been impure with children left in my care. My God has deserted me and I can't say I blame him. I have..." And then he began to weep uncontrollably and lay moaning on the floor at John Little's feet."

John Little brought Father Bachet back to his house, threw him in the bath and gave him a clean shirt to wear – albeit one he didn't care too much about.

Chapter 19

The old mountain man sat in the corner of the Denver railroad station. He smelled like hell, the wolf skins that covered him all stinking and ripe from walking a hundred miles in the autumn sun. John Little sat down as close to him as he could stand.

"Any idea when the next train be coming through, Mister? My horse is dead."

"I believe there is one coming directly," said John Little.

"So I was right. This is a train station?" asked the mountain man.

"Damn straight," said John Little.

"I thought so," said the mountain man. Came in here to sit for a spell, take a load off of my feet, about an hour ago, I reckon. Ain't seen no trains, though. But one coulda come by while I was a sleeping, I suppose. I once slept through a buffalo stampede, only woke up when one of 'em stepped on my damn foot - lost two damn toes to that critter."

"Sorry to hear it," said John Little.

"I rode into Denver to see this here poet," he continued. "Never seen no poet before. Seen Sioux Indians hang by cords stuck right through their chests for days on end and I seen fish that could fly like birds and bears that can dance, so I figured before I head back out to the Rockies again I might as well see what this poet looks like."

"And what poet do you speak of?" asked John Little.

The mountain man pulled a faded handbill from inside his skins and handed it to John Little.

"Looks more like a mountain man than some poet if you ask me," he said.

John Little looked at the rough drawing of Walt Whitman flabbergasted.

When the seemingly endless train journey that Walt Whitman had started in St. Louis finally arrived in Denver, he disembarked ever so slowly from the train, sure he would never stand up straight again, and the paralysis in his right leg which had disappeared some years before seemed to have come back with a fury.

"I could have celebrated myself more comfortably in Camden, New Jersey," he said to no one in particular as he disembarked and beheld the less hardly metropolitan view of Denver before him.

That evening he gave a short reading in the Birdsong saloon where chairs had been set up for the occasion. Of course, John Little sat right in the front row, transfixed by Whitman's sad eyes, the poet's beard longer and whiter then he remembered, as he read from the pile of his books stacked next to him. An aide had been selling copies of *Leaves of Grass* by the saloon entrance that quickly sold out when John Little bought every copy. He planned on putting the books in the pews of his church instead of Bibles.

When Whitman finished his last poem and thanked the audience for coming there was silence; it was not clear whether shock or misunderstanding was the cause, but then John Little stood up and began to clap loudly and Father Bachet sitting next to him did the same, and when others saw him standing there, tears running down his eyes in a state of ecstasy, they joined in heartily and soon all were on their feet applauding the old poet who stood shakily holding the lectern for support, truly amazed at this reaction.

Chapter 20

Qwing So was hardly speaking to her husband today. For weeks they had been arguing about the rights and wrongs of the recent embarking of General Pershing's American troops to Europe, joining the French and British in the meat grinding trench war with Germany, already three years old. John was saying that somebody ought to show that *fils de pute* limp-armed Kaiser that he couldn't be sinking the Lusitania like a toy boat in a gilded bathtub (of which John supposed he had many in his castle in Berlin) and if it had to be the U.S. who was gonna teach him a lesson, well so be it. Qwing So would quietly respond to his ravings that men loved to go to war no matter what side they're on or who is right or wrong and that Americans especially were always ready to show a thing or two to just about anybody who doesn't speak their language or share their color of their skin. But without admitting he was somewhat hypocritical to Qwing So, John knew he wouldn't ever want his dear son Victor to go over there or anywhere else to fight and maybe be killed for whatever the reason. John knew oh too well what a man looked like after he got shot - he had shot enough men himself - and the thought of his own boy turning pale as the blood drained out of him made him quake with repulsion.

Retirement had come early and easy to John Little and he was now quite content to spend his days just messing around the house, reading books and taking a short walk into town after lunch before napping in the afternoon. Once some dime novel journalist had come all the way from

Philadelphia to approach John Little about writing his *memoirs*. In fact, the man had nearly written them for him already, but John said he had too much respect for the written word to put his own name on such balderdash.

"But I could make you the most famous gunman whoever lived," pleaded the journalist. "I mean who else but you survived a hanging?"

"Not sure if I did survive any of it really," said John Little cryptically. "But it wouldn't be fair to Walt Whitman, you know, God rest his soul."

"Friend of yours?" asked the writer. "Outlaw of some sort?"

Good God man!" Cried John Little. "Walt Whitman lived and died in Camden, New Jersey, just across the river from your own hometown of Philadelphia and you're telling me you never heard of him?"

"Can't say that I have," said the writer, who like most Americans of the time, had no idea who Whitman was. "But I've already come up with what I believe to be an excellent title for your memoirs," the writer spread his hands dramatically in front of him. "Tell me if this doesn't make your hair stand up on end: *JOHN LITTLE - LAST OF THE MANKILLERS or THE SCENT OF BLOOD AND MONEY ON THE FRONTIER TRAIL.*" There was a moment's hesitation and then John Little started laughing hilariously and sent the disappointed man away without another word. He could barely remember all the men he had shot and killed and besides he didn't want to spoil his new identity in Denver. Of course, there were always rumors afloat as to who he might really be, but since the law wasn't searching for him as they had been for Jesse James, when he was living in St. Jo, Missouri under the alias of Mr. Howard, John had been able to keep his real identity largely quiet and his guns long retired.

He decided to mess around down in the cellar, ostensibly looking for a book he thought he remembered buying about the Austro-Hungarian Empire. Upon opening a large old trunk he came across the wooden six-shooter he had made as a boy, the one he had pointed up at Judge Durand when he stood and spat over his dying father. He could hardly remember his father's face anymore, just a fuzzy memory of him laughing over the dinner table about something that happened during the Civil War; only his laugh was left, everything else gone to dust but finally that was enough because the faces of his own child had replaced it. He held the toy gun up in his hand, so small now, so many real guns since then filled with bullets exploding in their chambers traveling down the length of the barrel and crossing the air and landing in a man's chest or stomach or head and ending a life, intruding into a space God never intended them to, he supposed. Then John felt the sharp pain in his own chest and in his elbows and up his arms and had an idea what was coming; he managed to sit down on the dusty chest before the vice grip around his torso became unbearable, the black dizziness behind his eyes closing in on him, slowly sliding down to the floor, his head resting against the chest. He was thinking that he was glad he was down on the floor already, he wouldn't want Qwing So to find him all banged up from falling and landing on his face. His breathing didn't connect anymore and he couldn't tell if he was conscious or not. He thought of his mother down in that root cellar in Old Oklahoma so many, many years ago and the thought of that was painful enough to make him die at last and then he wondered if Teddy Roosevelt had thought of him when he proclaimed Oklahoma to be a state in 1907. And then he was dead, gone from this world.

Qwing So found him a few hours later with the toy gun gripped in his hand, his head back against his mother's old wooden chest. She knelt in front of him and caressed his graying hair, his still smooth face, this boy-man she had crossed the country with, a gentle man who had made his fortune taking men's lives. And than she wailed in Cantonese, rocking back and forth on her heels until her children arrived and took her away.

The funeral for John Little was held on New Years Eve 1917. There were rumors in Denver that Theodore Roosevelt might attend but he never did show. Willie O'Keefe, the illegitimate son of Uncle George and Nell who had taken the family business to heart, served free drinks all day and dressed his thirteen girls in their finest black velour. And then Willie O'Keefe gave each girl two hundred dollars and a ticket to San Francisco. Himself, he took the stage to Washington DC and was talking about buying an ambassadorship from the new administration to some small Central American country where to kill or to be killed by an evil man was a way of life.

Some time later, when Qwing So was going through saddlebags and

239

trunks full of John Little's personal effects, she came across a faded and yellowed piece of old newspaper, folded and tucked into the corner of his thick wallet, barely legible, with a short phrase scribbled in smudged black ink. It was the same piece of paper that the boy Petit Jean had taken from his mother's hand that terrible night in Vendee when she lay drunk in their root cellar and he had carried it with him all those years since:

"Great is wickedness...I find I often admire it just as much as I admire goodness."

It was clearly signed *Walt Whitman*.

About the Author:

Living in Paris for over 20 years as an expatriate New Yorker, veteran rocker and author Elliott Murphy continues to have a very active career in music and literature. He has released over 30 albums, performs 100 shows a year and is a prolific author of fiction. Nearly four decades have passed since the release of Elliott's ground-breaking first album AQUASHOW (1973) (recently called an "Album Classic" by the prestigious UK magazine UNCUT and his 2012 CD JUST A STORY FROM NEW YORK was recorded during his triumphant return for a sold-out hometown show at Rockwood Stage in New York City. This live album follows his highly acclaimed NOTES FROM THE UNDERGROUND (2009) and ELLIOTT MURPHY (2011), which both received 4 stars on the prestigious All Music Guide. Elliott began his career with a troubadour like odyssey in Europe including a bit part in Federico Fellini's film "Roma." Returning to the US he quickly secured a recording contract and following the huge critical success of his first album came LOST GENERATION (Produced by Doors producer Paul Rothschild), NIGHT LIGHTS (featuring Billy Joel), JUST A STORY FROM AMERICA (featuring Phil Collins and Mick Taylor) and an extraordinary duet with Bruce Springsteen on SELLING THE GOLD (1996) who often invites Elliott on stage to perform with him during his European tours.

Murphy is also a published author of numerous collections of short stories, the most recently being CAFÉ NOTES and two novels COLD AND ELECTRIC and the neo-western POETIC JUSTICE. His fiction has appeared in Rolling Stone (U.S.) and other publications.

Photo: Françoise Viallon-Murphy

www.ingramcontent.com/pod-product-compliance
Lightning Source LLC
Chambersburg PA
CBHW060549260626
47161CB00003B/1127